PATYALA DOWN DE THROAT

...A sweet melody from pegs to riches

PATYALA DOWN DE THROAT

...A sweet melody from pegs to riches

Chandraprakash Mohata

Srishti
PUBLISHERS & DISTRIBUTORS

SRISHTI PUBLISHERS & DISTRIBUTORS
N-16, C. R. Park
New Delhi 110 019
srishtipublishers@gmail.com

First published by Srishti Publishers & Distributors in 2010

3rd impression, 2011

Typeset in AGaramond 11pt. by Suresh Kumar Sharma at Srishti

Printed and bound in India

This story is dedicated to
All those hostelites...
Who believe?
"It's my kinda type.

Especially **'THE EDIoTS'**

Acknowledgements

God, is the one to whom I owe this book. I am neither a professional writer nor an old player in this field. I am a simple human being but what seems special is the Person within me. He is a real Hero for me who made my goal of writing a success. He was the one to believe that I can write and so at every phase of this work he guided me professionally. You know who he is? He is none another than the Almighty.

However, there are certain mortals also who have lent their hand in this story, and they hold an important place in my heart.

One such is V.G. Patel, the founder director of EDI for creating this '8th Wonder' a platform to learn the art of entrepreneurship.

Then there are Friends from the 8th and 9th batch who gifted me the best story of their time to be conveyed and fulfill my purpose. My Professors, Staff members, & Mess authorities of Edi made my journey at Edi the most memorable one. In particular, Vivek Singhal, Ronak Modi, Abhinav Daga, Shiven Parthsarthy, Sillu (Tea vendor), Ankur Nahar, Gaurav khadiwala, Nilesh sonaje and Sumit Grover.

'Pooja' my wife to whom I owe special thanks for being with me as a true friend, giving suggestions about my work and improving my writing skills.

'Manoj Jethaliya', a friend of mine who has been with me through out my venture.

A friend, Philosopher and Guide, the 'three-some combo pack', i.e. Amit Bhatia, Harsha Ramchandani and Dr. Shalini Grover became the soul of my novel without whom I am incomplete and so would be the book. To Sudha Mehta I owe special mention for doing that revision task at a greater leisure.

My parents Esp. my mom Mulidevi Mohata, my brother Manmohan and sister Radha toshniwal who has been supporting me through out my life now seems immortal to my eyes.

My father in law Ram Ratanji Kothari who trust me believed Maji sa (holy worshiped god) would become a sole to this novel.

More of a friend than a publisher to me, Jayanta Bose has fulfilled my dream by putting his trust in my work and entice people to read my thoughts. He is one of a kind you will rare to find in this world.

Finally, myself, for without me this book wouldn't have existed.

Prologue

"Life is all about how you define and design it."

Those are the happiest moments of our lives, when you, by your own will, make them beautiful. Those moments, which do not give you the pleasure but act as hurting factor, become sad moments.

Therefore, it is all upon us, how we can make the best, out of our living. Nevertheless, is it possible to do so?

In this today's world, very few people live life the way they want to. I have just one question in my mind.

How many of you have spent one full day lavishly on your own wish?

I mean living life king size, giving others a damn about attitude, a matter of twenty-four hours, doing whatever your mind says, whatever your heart speaks!

The answer may be hundreds amongst millions who cannot live as per their wishes.

We join hands to pray, asking about the fulfillment of all our wishes.

However, does that happen?

We call ourselves free, despite of the fact that we are not.

Where relationship matters a lot, we are getting our selves chained. It is a trap, which we have imposed on ourselves by connecting our life to many other lives. These lives are none other than our family, friends, social circle, relatives, as well as the people who are directly or indirectly related to us.

Those people play an active role in defining what we have to do instead of what we want to do. Under such circumstances, its beauty becomes a misery, and we have no other option left behind us.

Our life isn't a result of a cheap bottle of wine or the full moon or the heart of the moment but to be very specific, we are a combination of precious genetic material. It's a gift from the day we are born till the day we pass on. But people around us demand sacrifices each and every time we wish to do something else in life.

This point tempted me to think why it is so that, "Can't I spend one single day of my life the way I want to?"

We are all, I suppose behold to our parents- the question is how much?

The question was tough but the toughest part was its answer.

Like every individual, I was also going through the same tough time holding a bachelors degree in business administration in one hand and a tensed thought in my mind on the other.

What should I do next was a big question for me like every other graduate. I just had four options. It all seemed like life was playing a KBC game with me.

A. Job with zero experience *(but who will give me a job)*

B. Join daddy cool with his business stuff *(and an early marriage and kids and...)*

C. MBA (sleepless nights and a hundred entrance exams)

D. "What Next?" with a big question mark

Phone a friend sounded the best lifeline for some interesting tips. Therefore, I called my brother to discuss about my issue.

Tring tring ... tring...

"Hey brother how's you," I greeted Birju Bhaiya with a smile.

"Everything is fine here. ICFAI is cool, the best among all. So how is you knee, he whispered in a low tone showing some pity on my condition.

"Knee injury is bad. Very bad!"

Because one eats a lot and sits, idle. However, you know the main problem is not in eating; it's in shitting and sitting as well.

"So what you thought," he started making a serious environment.

"Thought ... what", I whispered.

"About the career stuff, stupid!" He shouted.

You are already done with your bachelors and now did you plan anything regarding your masters?

"Please not now! Do not start it again. I am already screwed up lying here the whole day," I shouted in pain.

Actually, I wanted to talk but the pain was unbearable.

"You got a lesson to learn. So better, control your speed," he laughed gleefully

"It's the fiftieth time I have heard this since last Tuesday."

It wasn't only he who was pampering me with the typical one-liner but everybody else in house was following his path.

It is just a knee injury. Next time if you exceed above 100kmph, I bet you will end up loosing your life and there will be nothing to replace against it.

"Thanks for the advice! I will keep a check on my speed to 90" I laughed gleefully.

"Why don't you prepare yourself for the CAT exam coming November"? He questioned placing a detailed curriculum about the exam

"Hmmm ... Actually, I am planning to do something else."

"What ...? You and something else doesn't fit in my dictionary. I mean you wanted to do bachelors in business administration so you did and then suddenly skipping out masters is a crazy idea."

"I don't know, but not MBA, as there is no scope in this - at least for me."

Why ... no scope? There are many reputed B-Schools in India and I don't think getting in any one is tough for you. It only needs preparation and practice for the entrance and then you are in.

"It creates more managers than successful entrepreneurs," I said passing my statement with a confident tone. "I want to come into business line."

"I think the accident has affected your brains. You have already screwed up your career by not turning up for the SYMBIOSIS interview. Only a lucky person gets this opportunity.

"This accident has screwed up everything," I said.

My brother seemed more worried than I myself was, may be because he wanted me to be like him, well placed in a B-School like ICFAI Hyderabad.

I didn't even want to go there, so no regrets, I muttered. "Listen Bhai, I don't want to indulge in all these MBA programs.

"Jobs are not meant for me."

"So you have made up your mind to drop the idea of doing masters," he asked.

No... Not at all. I just want to be a part of such a program, which makes me learn something practical, something that is not related to books but to the field I want to go in.

"Join Dad! He will make the best of you. This will train you and make you efficient enough to handle the business stuff.

"But why, Dad? Do you think he could spare a minute from his business schedule? He is already busy with his work and secondly I want to do something new, something independent and not waving behind him handling his work."

"New business venture"?

Yes something new, which is of my interest where in I have the authority to decide and give a shape. Then only I can explore myself.

"If that is so, why don't you go to EDI?"

"EDI ...? Sounds strange, I heard it for the first time," I murmured inquiring about the new word.

"Sometimes when entrepreneurs are not born, they have to be created." Edi as a sole player performs the purpose of this creation.

"That's fantastic," I shouted in excitement.

"But when is the entrance exam? How to get in Bhai? I am confused about the material. What should I read? Were a series of questions I threw on his mind to answer?"

At last, there was an answer. "A boon..." which acted as a solution for my career, freedom, and wishes.

My brother showed me a true pathway, which I was looking for. However, it was difficult to convince him because he always wanted me to do my masters from Institutes like IIM or SIMBI. With a rough preparation, I gave the entrance exam. It wasn't easy but the most difficult part was its GD. When you are placed in front of a panel of management gurus, it's really hard to stop the sweat flowing from your forehead.

Friday the thirteen is a very unlucky day. There are myths about the date but for me the day became special when I received a green signal to enter the gates of Edi.

ACT 1

Are you ready for a roller coaster ride?

Ladies and Gentlemen, with a quick refresh, fit in your seats and jam your seat belts because now I am going to take you to– "The odyssey"

Do you know what it means? "A long adventurous journey."

Straight on the road to the heart of Gandhinagar, Edi where a soft natured boy came, completely new to the world seeking a solution to the questions bursting inside his head. But you know the story isn't about that boy but those 56 Ediots who turned up at Edi with a couple of dreams they wanted to turn into reality.

I, myself "Devendra Rai," one amongst those idiots' *opps...* Ediots who left home to live in a place all surrounded by forest. I wasn't scared of the place rather was happy to be a free bird. It was the time when I had recently recovered from a knee injury after five continuous months of bed rest.

Fucking bed rest! Which I hate the most. I was feeling my life to be a Kamasutra sequel with every month passing by. Wherever I was in I always gave an example of a fucked up looser. I don't know why I am boosting myself but whatever happened couldn't be blamed on god at least.

Vroom. Vroom. Dhoom...... Dhadam...

All I remember, when I could hardly open my eyes was the lovely face of the girl with red dupatta. I was following her at full pace of my bike in John Abraham style. But now, what I could see was everyone in white and I soon realized that I have ended up in the hospital again. Doctor was talking to dad about the fractured knee.

This was the fifth time in four years, thus the average worked out to be more than an accident a year.

Soon friends and relatives followed with fewer flowers and more suggestions. Hundreds of accident cases were been discussed in front of me, which sounded purely being taken from one or the other Hindi movie.

The talks just concerned with problems of today's youth, rash driving, and their carelessness for their career. All these talks were more disturbing than the fatal knee injury."I didn't give a thought that this injury would disturb me so loudly.

But, now I was there at Edi walking on my own legs with many expectations to be fulfilled...

2nd July 2006...

Tears were falling from my mother's eyes while packing my bags. I was about to leave home for Edi, not for a day or a month but as a resident student for one complete year. Though college was, just 18 km away, even then dad thought that would be better for me to be a resident there.

I was happy to celebrate the first anniversary of our matched thoughts.

All was well and good in life. May be the knee injury acted as a boon for me. Mom was acting as if I was going abroad. You know na… typical moms.

She packed eatables, clothes and things of utmost necessity as well as the things, which were not at all required. *Thepla's, Mathrri, Methi puri, Sev puri, Tamtam puri, Farsi puri, Gaund pak and Bikaneeri Bhujia* was some of the *Gujarati* stuff occupying the menu.

What can one do? After all, she was a mother. The care of a mother can never be forgotten because only when you are away, you miss her all the time. It was time to pray before leaving.

Mom says, "Blessings makes life tension free," but I always believe in myself. If you are true and your acts are wise, God's blessed hands will always be on you.

I left home with mom and dad, towards Edi. It took forty-five minutes to reach college. Mom believed that Dad was a bullock cart driver in his previous birth.

We entered the college gates on which it was written in bold letters. "ENTREPRENEURSHIP DEVELOPMENT INSTITUTE OF INDIA."

Security men seemed like two gargoyles guarding the entrance.

Everybody wish to see heaven but nobody wants to die. I saw

heaven here at Edi. 'It was a rainy day'. The rain has mellowed to a mist.

I felt a drop on my forehead. Then, on my cheeks. I could feel the freshness flowing with the breeze. Edi was just as I had imagined.

"Beautiful... bravo", I whispered in a soft low tone.

It is not always a woman who is called beautiful. She is just a fake beauty fading day by day. How I define beautiful *is "All those things in this world which we see, whom our eyes feel and the mind admires just the way our heart says so, are beautiful for me."*

I took my cell phone out of my pocket and clicked a picture of the nature's fascinating beauty. Then I turned and snapped a few of the institute.

"It was a perfect Edi day."

A journey of thousand miles began with my single step, which I raised inside the institute building and then after every step I raised, was making me feel much better and better that the feel resulted into a cute smile on my face.

My mother was looking at me. A smile crossed her lips too.

I could see the happiness in her eyes because after 5 months she saw the same jolly face, which she was eager to see.

I moved on the passage towards the reception counter where we countered with an angry old man. He was mad on the sweeper for not cleaning his table.

"Mr. Chattergie", my father called I don't know whom. I asked him whom he was calling as nobody has seen him before. That day I realized sometimes fathers can be stupid. "If some one kind of Mr. Chattergie would be there present in the group he would respond", he said.

"Oh! Hello sir… hello", a weird looking fat guy came forward boasting of him self being Mr. Chattergie.

I glanced out into the reception area, where my parents were naturally hanging on Mr. Chattergie's words like a cat on a rope. He gave me the hostel room keys and described about the institute. While he was speaking, I was lost in his words dreaming about those 290 days, which I was about to spend as a resident student in Edi. I was going to live in a wonderful world that was full of beauty, charm, and adventure.

"Have a good day!" Was what I heard from him who winded up the meeting with these last words?

The facilities were mind blowing, much like for some V.I.P.

Separate computer lab with 24 hours net facility, library filled with thousands of books for book lovers, a separate volley ball court and a badminton court, security guards every where, the greenery and the restricted areas created such a 'wow' effect amongst students that made them think Edi to be the 8th wonder. After all, when you are served like a Maharaja, who is not going to like it? This, too, is no surprise.

We shifted the luggage to my hostel room. The room grows so quiet; I could hear my own pulse.

"Oh my god, is it a hostel room or a hotel", my mom passes a surprising sigh. A one-of-a kind brown leather chair, a flat screen television hanging on the wall: a glass case along with an almirah beside to be filled with books and notes. More over attached bathroom split air condition separate beddings and study table were a few leisure's occupying the room.

"We will also get one of this kind", my mother pinched dad showing the coffee maker. "I think that came imported from china".

"Ok beta it's time to leave. Take care of yourself. Study well and live your life".

When my dad was giving his chore of advice, he pretended as if he was sending me to Vegas for a holiday trip. Mom cried for two reasons. Firstly, the "*Lambi Judai*" factor was making her depressed, after all, I was going to stay away from her, and secondly, she was very much inspired from those "*Saas-Bahu*" daily soap serials that she could not control her emotions and busted out in tears.

I changed my clothes and came in a *Hawaii Mood.*

A sandal, shorts, along with a funky T-shirt was the best outfit to chill in that weather.

So there was I sitting lavishly with legs spread wide open, with a home alone feeling. Nevertheless, I wasn't alone because while I was acting smart, daddy cool already came out with a smartest solution. After all he was my father and how could I under estimate him.

Breeze started blowing fast. I think it was an indication for a storm to come. I shivered and zipped my t-shirt up to my chin.

Suddenly the door of my room opened with a bang on the wall. The bent old trees too shivered due to the wind.

The sky had turned dark, so I could not see the face properly. I took a deep breathe and waited for my eyes to adjust to the darkness. A moment later, I heard the door open and close, and the knife-slice of the cold air that comes on his heals. My eyes grew wider with the fear as the person standing at the door gazed around the tiny, dark room.

Glancing up, my eyes caught a dark figure standing at the door. He raised his dark brown eyes towards me.

A strong gust of wind fluttered his hair.

A few moments of silence prevailed. I thought it was a dream. But to my surprise, a boy of small structure stepped inside the room.

I puked, "Raju you!" I screamed in shock. "What are you doing here?" I made a disgusted face.

I had a strange feeling looking at him. A bad feeling.

I saw his luggage and understood the whole story. Dad was very smart, as he did not let me know that he was sending a spy behind me. I had no clue that Rajesh Jhawar, my cousin was also going to join me at Edi.

"That's why I thought, how dad was convinced so easily for me to be a resident student," I murmured to my self.

"Hellooooooooo"! Where are you lost Bhai? Rajesh said while waking me up from that horrible dream.

"Come on brother! Get in," I continued. "But how come you are here?" I asked him about his sudden plans.

"After an unsuccessful CAT experience, it was much more difficult for me to get admission in a reputed MBA college," Rajesh muttered giving a dumb expression.

"So! — why didn't you try it again"? I said moving towards his shadow.

"As opting a job was not my cup of tea, learning the art of entrepreneurship was the best option I had," he said taking a deep breathe.

I wondered as if he was doing a Baba Ramdev exercise.

"That's, great!" I welcomed him with a sinking feeling inside.

He gazed outside the window, looking at the breeze, which was getting wild. He then continued with his words.

"After all people spend their entire life to get admission in IIM's for gathering knowledge and intelligence so that one day they could start of their own, thank God we are naturally born so."

That was a smart statement from a typical Marwadi.

I helped him shifting his luggage. "What"...! Why are you staring at me?" Rajesh whispered.

"It's heavy and lumpy too. What you have dumped inside?" I shouted.

"A few mouth watering stuffs to increase your kilos," he laughed throwing the empty bottles over the almirah.

The work occupied two complete hours to settle but after that we didn't event find a mosquito to kill.

"When you need fun, you need a company to enjoy the charisma of fun, to share and to feel it."

With this idea, we two went outside to explore.

"So"... (Pause)

"What are you peeping around brother"?

"Just the shit of your asshole, I am looking where it actually fell," I answered with a nasty expression.

At that moment, we met Vivek and Vishal. I moved to have a casual introduction.

"Hey boy, Wassa ... Up?" I called Vivek attracting his attention. He was close shaven, and it looked as if his moustaches had not been shaved, but been pulled out by the roots.

"Everything is fine! It was a hectic journey." he glittered.

"So you both are cousins like us"? I said applying my logic.

Actually, this is what I am bad at because illogical things always come in my mind first.

"No ... Nooo, not at all" he repeated.

"We both met in the train," Vishal interrupted in-between.

"Okay then! See you; catch you later and I started to move towards my room.

"OOps! Sorry I forgot you name," I murmured from behind scratching my head.

"Hey dude, it's a very old formula, better apply it on girls," Rajesh giggled with a surprise note from behind.

"Hi! I am *Vivek Singhal*, age 27, a *Haryanvi from Punjab* and meet him, he is *Vishal Bhatia* from *Gorakpur*," he replied.

"Dude! Your specification of age smells of something fishy inside your mind."

"So, you got it!" He laughed.

"Better, obey me because I am the eldest of all", he said and started to play with his mouth organ. I think at that time he was showing up his style statement.

"Fuck you man, there is Sameer Patel the eldest of all," I informed him.

"How old is he"? He questioned

"We will celebrate his 39th birthday this sixteenth," I announced.

"What the fuck man," Vivek giggled. What is he doing here with the students of his son's age"?

I laughed at his lame joke.

I suddenly had a strangest feeling – that I have met him before. Seemed, as if we were brothers in our previous birth. The feeling stayed for long but suddenly broke when...

"Okay then, need to have a bath." Vishal again interrupted in a hurry.

"Boss! If you have patience, you will get a natural shower within an hour," I said.

They both departed laughing at my comment.

It seemed strange about Vivek who came to Edi from such a long distance just for a stupid one reason he told to me. "Brother! My dad was after me to get married to Rekha auntie's daughter. You can say that I succeeded to skipped my marriage plan in the name of entrepreneurship"

That was the worst joke I have ever heard in my life.

Any way destiny wanted us to meet, so we were together at Edi. He fascinated girls with his moves, impressed them with his words, amazed them with his knowledge, and raised them in love with his charms. That was a kind of buddy he was. Born with a triple — "O" certificate (*Only One and Original)*. It's difficult to digest this trailer but trust me; I have actually watched the movie.

The first day started very nicely with these four friends. Amongst four of them, Rajesh, Vivek, and Vishal were the three.

"So," who was the fourth one!

Aha! How can I miss telling you about this buddy boy who was born with a golden spoon?

Ritesh Patel a dude straight away from Surat. His room was next to mine. I was amazed to see the chaos around which suddenly got visible with Almost 23 grim looking people who came to drop the boy. I felt his neighbors turned up to see him off.

After all Patel's don't need reasons to hang out.

But swear to god if it would have been in his parent's hand, they would even leave a care taker.

After an hour, Rajesh and I caught Vivek asking him to join us at the computer lab. With Vivek and Vishal, Ritesh also joined us as he too didn't find mosquitoes to kill.

It was in a short time we had made ourselves comfortable with the computer machines; a bomb shell babe attracted our attention with an interruption. She seemed pretty with a perfect ten. Long hairs, sharp nose, thin lips twisted in a snarl.

"Hi, I am Vanshi," she said softly. Her voice seemed floating in the air like musical violin

"Have you used blue lady?" Vivek interrupted in between.

"Wa...ht! Do I smell like that"? she said twisting her nose on sudden question of his.

"Of course! I have a dog's nose," he said sniffing showing his expertise to catch the odor.

"One, that's havoc and two, don't flirt around"

"That's strange!" He exclaimed. "I can't be wrong to judge the odor of the perfume."

"Can't you stop for a single second," she muttered.

"I haven't moved yet," he replied giving me hi-five.

"Stop! Will you? Otherwise I will bite you!" she screamed.

Vivek was an annoying boy. Meanwhile because of his conversation, she just forgot why she was there.

"So...! What brought you here," I asked diverting into a meaningful conversation. However, in the presence of jokers like Vivek how could one be successful!

"Actually, somebody has hacked my Gmail Id and I am getting a log in problem," she said in a tensed note. Suddenly I caught a glimpse of her key board and found that the caps lock button was on. I thought she was unaware about the thing.

"Hey look at…" the moment I thought to speak Vivek placed his hand blocking words to be uttered.

He signaled me to keep my mouth shut and play a prank. I tried to read the mischievous expression on his face. I wondered if Vivek was having the same funny thought, which I got with his company.

I presented Vivek, as a mastermind hacker with that triple 'O' certificate, for help. He took the charge and opened his bag. A USB hard drive, data cable and a few more gadgets occupied the desk. All these drama made him a perfect hero in my eyes.

"Hey guys! Please leave me alone and chat somewhere else," Vivek said, pointing towards the exit gate. We moved our feet's on his command but then, "hey Vanshi, please gimme your password", he called her from behind.

I saw a mischievous grin on his face. He moved his fingers on the key board and his grin grew wider.

"Hmm! Vivek has got serious with his work. Let's hang out!" I said.

We planned to move giving Vivek the computer and the password. Ritesh was more curious to watch a computer hacker performing his job.

"Hurry, Ritesh!" I tugged his sleeve pulling him out. "Move buddy," I told him.

"Wait"... He screamed peeping inside the monitor.

I gave him a gentle push. "Let's go." Finally, I had to bribe him with a dairy milk chocolate to get him out.

Ritesh lingered close to me. "You go first" he insisted making a fun.

We went to the refreshment center to have some chips and a chocolate for Ritesh. While we were sitting, I thought to increase my knowledge about the new girl Vanshi. Actually, it was cool to see her because finally we found a *she-goat* to trap for our time pass.

"So how are things moving at Edi?" Rajesh asked.

"What should I say? It's the first day only," she said while sipping her cola drink.

The softness in her voice was making me feel like a smooth hand moving over one's neck giving a current.

"But you can tell us about yourself at least," Ritesh said snatching the chocolate from me.

"I am *Vanshi Mehra from Jaipur, Rajasthan*. I live here with my grandfather Mr. Anand kishor Mehra the owner of Bansinath travels."

As soon as she introduced herself, Rajesh prompted showing a greedy Marwadi look, *"Aaila... Lottery."* After all, he needed a bike to hang around and god gave him the master key of 200 buses that were supposed to be assets of Bansinath travel agency. We busted out in laugh on hearing Rajesh's comment. It was now time to play the prank.

"Sooo...ooooo! Vanshi," I stretched the "O" word to give an effect.

"What do you think; will Vivek succeed in his task?"

"What a kind of question it is? It is difficult!" she explained, turning serious. "I wish he does."

I turned to Vishal to get everyone involved. What do you think of, Vivek? You were there with him in the train! Is he actually a genius or is he pretending to be genius?" I continued.

"What rubbish! I haven't seen him properly yet and you are asking me the size of his underwear!"

"Haaa... Aa ha!" Ritesh laughed with his mouth all wide open.

I gazed at Vanshi to place my final statement.

"Let's have a bet Vanshi. If Vivek succeeds, movie along with dinner from yo ır side."

"But what if he fails," she prompted.

"Anything! Whatever you say," I said.

"You guys will treat me at Taj Umed," she demanded placing her conditions. "After all you are five. Cant you spend this much".

"Rajesh will die with a heart attack," Ritesh giggled.

"Deal from my side," I said with confidence.

"Deal," Vanshi raised her hand for a firm shake.

I called Vivek and told him about the bet. As soon as I kept the phone down, he called back indicating all of us to come at the computer lab. He gave me a positive signal that the work was done.

"I— I, heard several gasps of surprise behind me", she turned back pointing at my cell phone with a spying expression.

We moved towards the computer lab to have a glance at Vivek's work.

"You did it so quickly"? Vanshi said giving a mixed expression. Her face looked as tiny and white as those distant moons that Galileo liked to spot in his telescope.

"Yap! It just took a few minutes to catch upon the rhythm," Vivek continued.

"Take a look"! He urged facing the monitor towards her.

"Wow. Cool!" I exclaimed. But, Vanshi glanced at me doubtfully.

Vivek was all-time smart. He had done his work quite a few minutes back but he paused for a while for the bumper prize announcement.

Ritesh jumped with joy because on the very first day he got a bonanza offer. Whatsoever the things may be, but that night we all went for "*Tokyo Drift*" sponsored by Vanshi.

Vanshi was a good companion especially Vivek's, who made a joke of her by acting as a palmist the next day. The secret behind the password scam was buried beneath our zipped mouth.

While that was our first day at Edi campus, the next day was going to be our first day in class.

At five in the next morning, the doors of my room opened. I don't wake up so early but it was Rajesh who wanted to practice yoga before class. I wondered why we need to get up when the sun hasn't. With the advent of the sun, darkness experienced a loosing battle. The sun spilled over my blanket. The rays were like a silk cloth giving a smooth touch. The excitement of first day took away the sleep from my eyes. I took my bath and got ready for the class.

As I entered, the class was 'Calm' and "Peaceful'.

A complete dark room, where lights had not occupied the place. The classroom was so silent that I could here my foot steps while moving down.

I stopped when I heard voices. The voices seemed to be floating through the hall. I switched on the tube lights. A white beam of light darted over the floor. It was surprisingly warm and silent inside, as if, some one had turned the knob and clicked off the sound.

Bright yellow light shone out from an open doorway at the end. I grabbed the middle seat to have a clear view.

While turning back, I saw students creeping in from the entrance door. I was looking towards individuals noting what they were doing, and how they were making themselves comfortable by finding the best place to sit.

Some students opted for front seats acting as if they wanted to be Newton's from the very beginning. Some students opted for corner seats so that they could feel the cold coming from split AC's and sleep well in class. Some students like me choose the middle seats because they always want themselves to be the center of attraction.

While I was still into looking at people creating their impressions in my mind, everybody else was looking at me creating their own perception about me.

I didn't see when our course coordinator Dr. Minakshi Pandey entered.

In order to escape from other's eyes, I stood up. A strong tough voice with welcoming words began to wave around the class.

"Good morning dear students," I am Dr. Minakshi Pandey your course coordinator. It's good to see new faces. On behalf of the director, I welcome you all to the Edi family. The professor started with a pep talk for encouragement, and then continued with a long list of instructions to be followed, what to, and what not to do at Edi.

"At the beginning, I would like to say a few things, which will make you clear that the PG program, which you are in, is not a one year paid holiday for you people", she proclaimed.

"You have to do whatever you are told and follow all the rules and regulations laid down."

Those words were creating a hammer effect in my mind. Her

voice echoed all around the class. Her sound boomed louder. It all blended becoming a roar, a roar that ran inside the whole classroom.

'A roar of horror', I wondered.

I was thinking, "If this is the situation on the very first day how could we innocent people bear our course coordinator for one year!"

She was trying to create her authority among the students so that they obey her. After some time she came out with a list of rules to be followed.

Rule one: 'Every one should be on time in class i.e. at sharp 9:45'.

Two: 'If anyone is found to be late, he or she will not be allowed to attend that particular lecture'.

Three: 'Any kind of "Misbehavior" or "Disobedience" will not be tolerated'.

Four: 'You have to sit on the same seats where u r sitting today. This will remain your permanent seats'.

The students who were sitting in the first row were regretting their impulse and those who wanted a good sleep were so scared that they suddenly switched off the AC's because now they suddenly started feeling cold.

It seemed that everybody was busy thinking....

"Boss... maidam bahut solid lag re li hai, aakha saal bamboo karke rakhegi"

Rule no. Five: "No cell phones in class." If any body's mobile rings in between the classes, it will be taken away and will be given after 7 days after consultation with the student's parents.

The list of rules was very long and I was getting bored. I felt like a kid sitting between the audiences. It was really bullshit. Nevertheless, what one could do, after all she was our course coordinator. Suddenly

Rule No. 5 clicked in my mind.

"If by mistake cell phone rings, it will be taken away for 7 days."

While she was describing the situation, I was really dreaming about that situation. I muttered to my self, "hey Dev, suppose your cell rings by mistake in class then what will happen...?"

"No cell for 7 days"...

"But what about *Nisha, Pooja, and Jyoti*"?

"How will you talk with those beautiful girls? How will you adjust your life for 7 days? "

"Seven days buddy! Seven days! It is a pretty long time." I continued brooding over the fact.

Haven't you seen the Hindi movie "Lage raho munna Bhai"?

It describes when every half second a girl gets a proposal from a boy. So there will be 2 in a second, 7200 in an hour, 72,800 in a day. It might be much more difficult for each girl to say no to 12, 09,600 probable proposals during these 7 days.

"Your probability remains just 0.000000827! Think about it man."

'Any questions'? I heard from my course coordinator's mouth after the end of her long list of rules and regulation.

Everyone peeped here and there after that threatening lecture. There were endless questions & thoughts, but silence in the room seemed to grow heavy.

No one moved. No one spoke. I felt as if the room was jammed with silent, grim looking people.

The rhythm broke when Dr. Pandey started speaking to wind up the session.

As soon as she ended the session and planned to leave, a hand raised and a voice came out from the middle. The hand was mine and I spoke out.

"Hello Ma'am! Good morning. I am Devendra Rai or Dev to be precise and I have just one question in my mind".

"Yes. Proceed! You may ask any doubt." She said being unaware of the stupid question, I was going to place.

"If the cell phone of an innocent person like me rings with no intensions to break the rhythm of class, what is the probability of not getting the punishment laid by you in rule no. 5?"

Actually, I was trying to consider both the probabilities. Everybody was looking at me while I was speaking. Those foolish words were so innocently spoken that it broke the serious environment created by Minakshi Ma'am by her own laughter. Every one laughed with her, with applause. I was on the 9th cloud on the very first day. I started a movement of fun and enjoyment by a radical change. The change was in our course coordinators behavior teaching that students could also be handled by being friends. The change was in class environment when everybody began to talk with each other. The change was in freedom of students where there were free to sit wherever they wanted.

After the session, a peon came to our class with a notice. The notice was about the next session. Everybody had to gather again at 2:30 after lunch near the conference hall. Hunger made me rush to mess. Mid way, Vivek and Vishal joined me. It was a buffet system. I took my plate and had a close look at the menu.

"*Is there any celebration today*? " I said above a whisper looking at the feast.

Mukeshji, the mess owner overheard what I said.

"Every day seems celebration here at Edi. You will be treated with such delicacies daily," he replied with a jolly note. My mouth watered dreaming about Mukeshji's words.

Khoya kaju, Paneer tikka masala, Mix vegetable handi, Dal Makhani, Pinaple Raita, Butter Roti, Russian salad, masala Papad, Pickles and Butter milk. - Slurp!

Now imagine about an educational resort like Edi, where you are provided with air-conditioned classrooms with stretchable revolving chairs, hostel rooms with attached bathrooms, individual wardrobe study tables, bed etc. Life seemed cool after all these facilities.

I had my lunch with new friends Vivek, Vishal, Ritesh, and Rajesh my cousin.

We rushed to our class at 2:20pm, after lunch, keeping in mind rule no.1. Prof B.B. Siddhiqui was taking micro lab exercise. It was some kind of psychological exercise to know each other better. Under this exercise of micro lab, a few individual had to share their strengths and weakness with each other. There I had a word with Sameer Patel who was the eldest among all students.

When you look at an individual, he may seem respectable by his age, attitude, and caliber but what you perceive is always not correct.

As each budding entrepreneur came from a different place, a new state, with his own cultural habits and attitude it was difficult to judge their caliber. Now let me introduce to a new personality whom we gave respect but because the outcome was negative, we took it back with interest.

He came from 'Mumbai' to Edi for various reasons: a practical exposure, one-year vacation from business life and a lot more. Being a senior student we used to respect him a lot.

The age, which we were in, he had already passed some years ago, so he was bound to get our respect. Assignments were less and activities were nil.

There Sameer Bhai started his feed back secessions. He thought that by giving negative feed backs one can develop himself.

But actually they simply indicated, *"Feed from back."*

When the discussions among friends took place, Sameer diverted them with his own thoughts. It is not giving suggestions but his feed back sessions were somewhat different. Most of the time he stressed on negative feedbacks where he could kick another individual's ass so easily with his words.

A wrong thing I mean. If you are, a senior that doesn't mean you can rule over a junior. He passed comments in such a way that others felt irritated and frustrated. One day he hammered me.

"You disturb the rhythm of class Dev with your jokes and that's not done with it," he said angrily. We are here to study and master the art," he continued. "So it's advisable for both of you, stop jerking around, and let others concentrate", he pointed Vivek placing his statement.

Vivek couldn't digest the insult and left the place in anger.

That night at 3 am Vivek called all the four of us outside Sameer's room. No body was sleeping so we thought to follow his intensions. A few minutes later, he brought a street dog and kicked her in Sameer Bhai's room. He then locked the room from outside.

We all laughed on this and left the place. At four in the morning different sound vibes came from Sameer's room. Everybody gathered in fear to know what has happened. When we opened the door, the dog came out barking loudly.

"Hey, Sameer what happened?" asked Rajesh.

"Fuck you asshole; I want to know who the hell left the dog inside my room?" he came out in frustration.

"Bull Shit! But what's this? Who is the third one?" Everybody laughed looking at the puppy.

The plan was working.

I was standing in the group of viewers. The doers of the prank were still sleeping. Actually when we left, Vivek again turned to Sameer's room and left a puppy inside.

It just needed a spark to light the fire.

"Oh my god! What did you do with the dog," I trembled. "You are disgusting," I pushed Sameer holding his collar.

"What I did"? He exclaimed in depression. A drop of sweat fell from his eyebrow with a sudden reaction of mine.

"If you were so desperate, you would have told me. I would have made some arrangements. Why to rape a dog?"

"This man has lot of potential," somebody from the crowd shouted.

"After all his reactive sperm gave birth to a puppy over night," Vivek interrupted rubbing his eyes.

"Congrats, dude! Now you are a father of a puppy. Take that as a positive feedback," I said. "But what will we name our uncle's daughter?"

"Simran Sameer Patel," again, somebody from the crowd shouted.

It was masala news to be discussed in the class. We boys were all prepared to fire the second round. In the class when it was time for our lecture to begin, I came up with a note as an announcement.

"Good morning," friends.

May I have your attention please? It has been a very grateful day for us today in Edi, as Kanta Bhabi has given birth to a puppy. When humans have reached to such a stage where over night births have started taking place, all the credit goes to our most experienced student.

It's an important day for Sameer Bhai and his daughter Simran.

Let me introduce you the newborn baby."

Meanwhile Vivek had dressed the puppy with his t-shirt and a small cap to give her a rich look. Above her tale it was tagged,

"A small token of gift to Kanta, love Sameer."

Vivek who was holding Simran made her sit on the center table. I continued further.

It's the happiest day for Sameer too. Very few people get the joy of being a father so fast.

So let us celebrate the day with a feast tonight.

Meanwhile, Rajesh had already talked with Mukeshji about the prank. He got ready to serve the dinner at main lawn.

Posters were displayed at different places specifying the below. Sameer in great frustration locked himself inside his room. He neither turned up for lectures nor for lunch.

After evening the dinner was arranged at the lawn. The notice displayed brought everyone to the feast. The arrangement was appreciated but people around were still unaware about the person behind the scene. Many thought me to be a prime suspect but I raised my empty hands upwards, to show my innocence.

Finally, Sameer Bhai got a lesson for his deeds. After dinner, everybody went to his or her respective rooms to sleep.

The clock showed 1am and I was feeling sleepy too.

I told Vivek about my sleeping plans but he still seemed unsatisfied with the revenge he took. He went to Sameer's room and found him in deep sleep. He came back to me and muttered a few words into my ears.

"Have you gone mad?" I whispered

"Yes, I have," he shouted and took out a fire cracker bomb from his pocket.

"Where the hell you bought that from?" I growled.

"A seasonal fire cracker shop," he said.

"But Diwali is not near by," I said scratching my head in confusion.

"Dude! You are in Ahmedabad since twenty years now," he reminded of my birthplace. "Don't you know that there are firecracker shops for seasonal marriages"? Vivek's voice remained just above a whisper.

"Ooh"! I nodded my head. Is that so?" I sounded like a fool.

He went to Sameer's room where he was sleeping tight.

"He might be dreaming about Kanta Bhabhi," I giggled. It was the worst idea to explode a bomb under his bed. At that point, of time when the night was silent and he was lost in sleep.

"He might die of a heart attack," I continued. "It's too dark," I complained turning back to him.

But, who could stop Vivek? He took out a match stick lit the bomb and threw it into Sameer's room.

PARTY @ EDI

For
The First Time
In the history of Edi

SOMBODY HAS CREATED A MIRACLE.
VERY FEW PEOPLE ARE CAPABLE OF DOING IT

&

SAMEER PATEL IS AMONG THE VERY FEW.

LET'S CONGRATULATE HIM
WITH A TRUE HEART

A KIND INVITATION FROM

SAMEER PATEL

FOR DINNER TONIGHT

EDI LAWN ☺ SHARP 8PM

Within few seconds, the bomb exploded with a loud noise and gave a 440-voltage shock to others.

"You — you scared me," I said letting out a shrill laugh. We managed to hide ourselves.

I glanced back. "Ohh"! A frightening moan escaped my lips.

Sameer was so sacred that he came out of his room with a shouting voice.

"Burn me mother fucker". "Burn me till my ash satisfies your soul" He repeated. A loud voice escaped Sameer's throat as he experienced the shock.

Anger glowed around Sameer Bhai like electricity. His mouth dropped and his chin started quivering.

The noise woke up every individual at Edi. Soon all gathered to see what has happened.

Sameer had gone mad as he started to beat his head with his own hands. His eyes glowed like burning coals as he glared up at the crowd.

I caught a glimpse of his face, a hard, angry face. He wrapped his arm around me and holds on as if he was loosing balance.

I thought we had crossed our limits to make fun of the scene in the name of revenge; I tried to utter something in a low voice. My voice trailed off looking at his condition. However,

Mumbling to myself. "What is going on here"?

"Are we nuts? Crazy and dangerous?"

I glared at Sameer merrily.

I put my hand on his shoulder to calm him. "Sameer! You will be fine," I said soothingly.

We almost screwed him up. I could hear Sameer's rapid breathing behind me. "Sameer—please don't get screwed up," I pleaded.

The security guards too came to see. "What happened"? The guards demanded nervously. They thought may be a short circuit had occurred. The night guard eyed us suspiciously. Vivek and I exchanged frightened glances.

"Let's get out of here," I said to Vivek in a trembling voice. With us the chaos too departed leaving the sufferer to suffer.

Sameer Bhai settled down a few days after the shock. He now gave positive feed backs only. I came in touch with new friends adding them in my cart.

Take my word, there is nothing like good or bad in a person. It is just our minds who makes a perception. Therefore, when Vivek, Ritesh, and Rajesh who neglected addictions like smoking drinking and tobacco were my company, I also began to spend quality time with addictive individuals like Shiven, Modi, and Sid. Amongst all, Shiven was the guy who fascinated me the most. Do not take me wrong. I am completely straight in this matter. I felt his characteristics were unique and that distinguished him as a Bindas boy from others. That day in the mess I got to know him more better.

Shiven made back door entry possible in reputed B-schools in Pune, Delhi, and Maharastra. He was a master in his job. His network was strong and earning a few thousands was his left hand game. His pocket occupied four cell phones, eight credit cards and a bundle of few thousands all the time.

"*Hey buddy!*" I greeted him in the mess.

"Let us see what is in the lunch," he replied with a hungry expression moving his hand over his tummy. "*Bhindi...* Eh! What kind of food is that?" I hate Bhindi he said making a Dracula expression.

"They are not too crazy about you either," I laughed looking at him.

"Next time I will tell Mukeshji to make special kebab's for you. Let us settle with the Bhindis today."

"No boy, not at all", he said. "Let's go out, but do you have a bike"? He tugged his hand on my sleeves pulling me hard.

Actually, Bhindi was not my favorite too. So, we moved out on Rajesh's splendor. We went to the near by fuel station. Now where to go was confusion for us.

"Who could compete with Taj Umed in the race of Excellence?" Shiven said.

"I think that is the best but quiet expensive," I said keeping the budget factor in mind. "Will go to Narayani" I exclaimed. "It's situated besides our college only."

"No will go to Taj," Shiven uttered.

"But Narayani serves quality food and we will get 10% discount in the name of Edi." While I was acting as an economical person, spoiled brat Shiven didn't bother to spend thousands to satisfy his hunger. I checked out my pocket to see the cash balance.

"Hundred, two... Three hundred and forty rupees more! That is what I have," I told him frankly before my day ends up washing plates for the hotel.

"Don't worry, I have the *Farzi* credit card (Bogus), we will eat lavishly." He said showing the illegal card he had.

"Bull shit! What a person you are!" I said glancing at the card.

"Don't you feel afraid of all such acts?" I asked

"Listen man! If you want to have the pleasure of coconut water either, pay the expense and have the pleasure or plug it from a coconut tree for free. I always opt for the second option."

I felt awkward to go at Taj on a bike. Nevertheless, when we had cash inside our pockets, the status symbol did not annoy us. We parked the bike aside and went inside. "So..., what will you have"? Shiven asked

"Anything will do," I said looking greedy. It was my 1st time in that marvelous place.

He ordered a wide range from soup to dessert. After all, it was a free lottery ticket.

"Why don't you save the income occurring from admissions"?

"Take my advice, it's good to spend the illegal money as soon as possible before any other claims for it", he replied.

"But why don't you invest in stocks," I said giving him a better option.

"I will choose to have lunch here everyday", he smiled sipping the soup. "There is no guarantee for this kind of money. So spend it before god snatches it from your hands." He continued.

"I believe one should save for the future. That's what I always do to create my balance." I said

"Can you pass me the Raita please?" he asked ignoring my words.

"Shiven! I said something," I muttered.

"Eat, drink, and have fun," he continued. "Do not get into all these bullshits. Why are you taking my headache on your self?"

I had never seen such a person. He didn't want to hear my rubbish, which I was talking. From my part, I tried to make him understand but there was no end to his adventures because for him life was either a daring adventure or nothing.

ACT 2

A series of unfortunate events

It was hardly a month at Edi when Vivek and Vishal brought some interesting gossip news to my ears. I saw their faces. They were something like of a person who has accidentally seen their maid bathing.

"What's the matter, why are you people so excited?" I said peeping down with eyes sunk inside a heavy lumpy Philip Kotler. I wondered if it's so difficult to read this how annoying would have been for the author to write.

"There is a mind blowing hottie in our campus. Long hairs, smooth and silky, milky white made up of cream – vanilla… ahhh.

"Hemmm…oh yehh, that sounds erotic but what's fishy about her"? I said loosing connection with the book which soon ended on the floor as if it was meant for somebody else.

Jasmine and you know what the best part is, "She stares at you man."

"What? She just stares at me." It felt like digging a gold mine till bottom and later on discovering shit debris inside. "What is fucking great in this"? I don't know what you guys get being a spy all the time. Every body stares! You stare, I stare, and she stares. There is nothing wrong about it. God has given us eyes to look around and see the view. If I am a view for her, what is the problem with you? It doesn't show that she is interested in me. You are wasting your time and my time too. Why don't you study instead of peeping here and there and gathering spicy news for evening every now and then?"

"Fuck man! Can't you keep your little john silent for a while and listen to the whole thing. We were on a project for a few days. We named it **"THE INSIDE STORY."**

Shall I ask you one thing? Have you ever noticed your surroundings when you speak in class, at the mess or in a computer lab?

"No... Not so carefully. But why should I"?

"Somebody is constantly watching you," he said as if dad has sent another spy behind me to keep a watch.

I can feel her looking down at you every now and then, as if you are some kind of creature she has never seen before.

Let me present you the report we have worked on to give you a clear picture."

Day 1....

You woke up at six and went to *Shillu* that tea vendor (There is Ram Bhai outside IIM, we had *Shillu* outside Edi) for the morning tea.

While, you were walking, did you notice a girl passing by?

She was moving fast but suddenly she slowed down. As she passed did you see her turning back? We saw that including Priyanka who was making a mischievous grin which girls generally do by twisting their nose.

At that moment, Vishal and I got a clue and we started working on this project. During breakfast time, she came too early. When we people entered, she had already finished up with her breakfast. I saw her plate. It said, “Will you eat me too”. She was just having unnecessary conversation with Sid, that fatso guy whom she doesn't know even. *When her plate was empty why was she still sitting?* You were in your own jolly mood. But, while her eyes were on you, our eyes were tucked on her.

In class, we grabbed our seats away from you. You were busy with the assignment stuff. This was the third time we caught her. She was more interested to see what you were doing.

“But how could she peep? I was sitting on the second row fifth seat corner left,” I said making a statement on their unnecessary hype.

Do you know where she places her round shaped ass?

Exactly, behind where you place.

Day 2....

It was a Sunday. We all were busy playing volleyball. Did you see how interestingly she was watching you when you were playing?

Her favorite sport is badminton but she has started taking interest in other sports too especially volley ball. Actually, I came to know about the favoritism thing during micro lab exercise by Prof. Siddhiqui.

She came for breakfast late because now she knew your time schedule.

Have you ever noticed?

"She has reduced the amount of bread slices to two with lots of butter inside because you always have the same"?

That day Priyanka asked me to go for a movie. For the first time she had a word with me so frankly and that too, directly a movie invitation. She wasn't inviting me personally but all of us and it was a clear indication.

Day 3.....

When you did not turn up for the break fast and even for the class, on Monday I saw her mood was bad the whole day. That day you were out shopping bikini's for your aunt's nephew.

At night, I could see her enjoying the music coming from your room. She was dancing off to the T.V room with joy. On the next moment, I played a hip-hop and she went away. My music was not that bad that she did not even mingle.

Day 4....

We were in the library. When we were gossiping, you were busy reading *Sidney Sheldon's The Other side of midnight.* She was also reading something but actually, she was much more interested in your interest.

Do you remember that I forced you to hang around at Shillu's place for tea?

When we left, I peeped from window after a few minutes. *She was actually reading the same Sidney Sheldon's book.*

Day 5.....

Our report finally got its charm when we attacked girl's hostel.

Vanshi helped us to get into her room. Though, it was risky but we had to get a conformation. Jasmine & Vanshi share a single wall so we could easily find something undiscovered.

Priyanka was teasing Jasmine by your name. The tease was in the form of a fantasy. I haven't heard a girl getting so naughty.

"What the fuck was it? Are you kidding? Are you nuts?" I said with a surprise. My stomach squeezed tight.

"No! Not at all. Ask Vanshi if you don't trust me." Vivek said pointing his middle finger indicating two things at a time. Either trust her or fuck off.

"No, I don't believe you; I think you are making fun of me." I said. May be its all your dream you saw yesterday night or a kind of grapevine you want me to believe."

"Do you doubt my work?

"Although I am not dumb enough to believe you but still I have to look over what you said".

I thought, may be Vivek was serious. The description was so real, but then, I had to confirm the news.

There began a journey where we friends decided not to disclose this issue and work on this new project from next day onwards to know whether this project could give a positive outcome or not?

Everybody wanted to disperse but something seemed to jog Rajesh's memory. He framed the next day's plan.

"If Vivek is so confident about his report let me check it again." Rajesh started to speak solemnly

Tomorrow guys, be ready at 9:30 am for class. As lectures starts at

9:45am, we should be the first one to grab the back bencher's seats. From now onwards let Jasmine struggle to catch her view. Pen down each suspicious act of her. The moment she will turn we will catch her red handed".

That was a fantastic idea and we all cheered with fun and enjoyment because the next day was going to be exciting. We made ourselves comfortable on the backbenches as we had decided.

It was 10 min for the class to start. I was writing something on the black board. I saw everybody had begun to come inside. Jasmine too entered with her friends Priyanka and Unnati.

"Hey Dev, can we have our pleasure to make you sit with us?" Vishal and Rajesh shouted.

"Sure why not!" I said and started to move towards them. I took a few baby steps so that I could see her with naked eyes the truth behind the illusionary story.

But as I was moving, her eyes meet mine as I passed her.

They were the darkest shade of black so surprising that when she stared at me I completely forgot what I was planning to do.

I looked at the shine of her flyaway curls and the butterfly flight of her smile. She was Smooth like vodka and hot like a spice, a mist so clear which give me a gentle stroke.

"If you don't concentrate on stairs, you will fall," Vivek shouted to make the girls hear his words.

Prof. Minakshi Pandey entered the class with a Pile of Economics material, which got to be distributed. Everybody got into the studying mood but my eyes couldn't stop thinking. Those beautiful eyes which clashed while passing by were not letting me concentrate. Vivek's story had started its effects. When you watch a Harry Potter movie it is very difficult to come out of it soon. Every time I tried to concentrate, her face grabbed my attention. I quickly lost interest in the subject while looking towards her. I haven't ever seen a girl so fair.

She moved her milky white hands and removed the clutcher that tied her hair. She bent her neck pulling her long brown hair out from under the collar. When she released her hair from its prison, I experienced the freedom which her flowing hairs were feeling.

"Wow. Is that real!" I murmured inside.

The freedom was in the form of words, which came out without any reason.

"The Mountain Girl...!"

She is not made of honey and yet so fair,
Heat melts her away but heat doesn't dare,
Big black eyes as a mermaid jus awoke,
A mist so clear which give my confines a gentle stoke,
My heart chills away and the body freezes out,
Emotions pore and ooze its feels like the ninth cloud,
That mountain gal her voice is so sweet,
That when she sings it is followed by natures greet,
Those shining and flowing hairs as if mothers care,
The falling river shy away and the eyes cant stop looking there,
Happiness enrobes the atmosphere and the Pandora's evil leave,
I feel like care for her more than any 1 believe,
My friendship resides for her and my goal is nothing besides her,
My life though no where near still always strives to be her,
Like the ray of light kills the darkness within a sight,
in the same manner her charm castled in enlightened night,
She chained ma heart and captured my thoughts,
her smile disarms me as it's says "forget me not",
Seasons came seasons left but still ma heart craves for her
I know my destiny strikes on me but still I will always wait for her

While I was writing those beautiful words, Ritesh called me. I was supposed to ask the reason but...

"Hey.... Hey you, stand!" the professor roared.

"Who? Me?" I replied shakily.

"Do you know what is going in the class?" I was silent and everybody was looking at me.

I stood hunched like a scarecrow, with my eyes vacant, face blank, as if my mind was somewhere else.

"Elasticity and its types madam, "that is what I saw written on the black board.

It's good that you at least know the topic. But do you know the meaning. I know you were not concentrating but busy doing something else while I taught the whole topic."

"No Mam, I was concentrating." I said with a low tone. She had a booming voice that thundered.

"If you think that you are smart enough to fool me then speak exactly what I thought."

Speaking on the topic was an easy task but speaking exactly on the topic was something like recreating 'The MONALISA' again. It now became a matter of self respect for me. Jasmine was as usual staring at me but I had no words.

There are some instances in life, which leaves a memory, and those instances play a very good role at time of needs. That is what happened with me.

Nirmal Soni's *five-ball theory* of elasticity suddenly peeped into my mind. He was my economics professor at IMS.

I started using some management jargons and his words in mind

"When you stretch elastic there is some change but who knows how much change has occurred?"

The responsiveness to this change in elastic by stretching is elasticity.

More over, I would like to present ***Marshal's 5-ball theory*** (though it was somebody else's) which will give a new idea to understand the topic and prove my sincerity in class. Consider five types of balls-tennis ball, a crazy ball, a supernatural boll, a cork ball, and a shot put ball.

Everybody was laughing at me by now.

I don't know how it came into my mind, but it was something that the professor also had heard for the first time.

I continued with my theory solemnly.

If you loose a shot put ball from a certain height say 1, you will see the shot put stick to the masses and does not bounce back. So elasticity equals to zero (e=0).

If you let loose a cork ball from a certain height it would bounce back half the height so e< 1

If you let loose a tennis ball from a certain height it will bounce back till the height so e=1

If you let loose a crazy ball from a certain height it will bounce back above the height it was thrown so e>1

If you let loose a supernatural ball from a certain height it will bounce back to the universe making elasticity equals to infinity."

Listening to my words with a mind-blowing example, everybody praised my knowledge and clapped loudly. However, they also knew that the theory was a stupid excuse to skip and not of marshal's.

They were clapping not for my knowledge but for my intelligence how impressively I presented and saved myself self-skip from Prof. Minakshi.

"Did you see today how carefully she was listening to you?"

"Where is she now"? I said turning my eyes to the view which I was eager to see.

"Don't..! As she is looking at you only," Vivek said giving me a quick review about her acts.

"'Are you sure, that she is interested", I asked taking a deep breathe. I wanted to look back but then I thought I trust him. 'So what should I do'?

"Now also I am telling you! She is interested. *"Sahi hai mauka mar de chokka."* Vivek said with confidence.

I was still in a trauma after listening to Vivek. It was difficult to ignore him because I myself felt the same while passing by her. Starting days were a bit enthusiastic. Later on laziness started to capture my mind and body. Lavish food with no labor activity and long sleeping hours made me feel a bit heavy.

For a few days, I neglected all this but when things went out of control, I decided to wake up early. Actually, the weight went out of control which I had to maintain in order to keep my TRP high at college. I could feel the fat lying on my tummy. The next day I woke up at six and went for exercise, wearing my jockey shorts and a nylon red t-shirt.

While I was jogging I encountered with two hot chicks.

"Hey there! Good morning," I was interrupted by a smooth, cool voice which fell into my ears. I raised my eyeballs to see who was there. It was Jasmine and Priyanka who also woke up early to have the pleasure of the beautiful morning.

"Hey, it's nice to see you here. How's everything?" I asked making a start for a conversation to begin.

"Do you wake up everyday so early?" Priyanka twisted her hair into a knot and holded it in place.

"No not at all. I saw you girls coming, from my room's window. So I thought why leave an opportunity when I got one to impress you," I laughed making a fun of the two.

"Oh, really!" Priyanka said giving a surprised look. "That would be so sweet if you would have done that."

"Shall I try something else or you girls are impressed," I again made a fuss.

"Hee ee…" Priyanka just laughed giving a break to the conversation but Jasmine didn't even grin.

"So…, "I started looking around. I had nothing more to joke now. I suddenly found myself running out of words.

"Yes so! (pause)…speak up", Priyanka spoke.

I twisted my mouth in a thoughtful pout.

"Actually, the jogging shorts are extra short which is making me feel embarrassed!" I replied making an innocent face.

I blinked and a laugh bubbled out of Priyanka. Even Jasmine cracked a smile but then she again turned to her silent mood.

I found that Jasmine was silent and only Priyanka was speaking. She was discussing about some college stuffs but I wasn't interested either. I was just staring at Jasmine's lips waiting for words to come. She was checking my patience but she didn't know that I become impatient in a very short time.

"So what's your name I forgot?" I applied the RJ's (Rajesh Jhawar) logic – "Better applicable on girls".

"I am Jasmine from Goa," she blinked at me. Then a slow smile spread across her face, as if she decided she just might like me after all.

While she was speaking, my eyes were staring at her lip's movements. Her voice created a rhythmic sound into my ears.

People say, "*Happiness is always short.*" The mood broke when another voice interrupted, "And you know me Na! Priyanka Mehta, a commerce graduate from H.L College?"

"Oh! That's great!" I said scratching my right ear. I forced a smile uncomfortably on my face instead of giving weird expressions.

Finally, crash of a romantic mood and dreams in vain...

"Hey, I am Devendra. My name isn't seems like one we always use to here in *Ramanand sagar's Ramayana – Devraj indra* uff *Devendra.*

"You are the same mobile guy na who seemed much worried about his cell phone," she said making fun of me.

"Ya, that mobile guy! So you remember that incident ha?"

"Yep she remembers every incident after all her memory is very sharp!" Priyanka said.

(Dear Readers: Did you see that? Girls are always like this – sudden & unexpected. The one who has to speak is always silent and the other one is a chatterbox.)

"Sharp memories... hem! So, are you comfortable here?" I asked Jasmine

"When there are fun loving people like you who will get bored?" Priyanka again interrupted. "Especially, when you brought Simran into picture, I felt pity for Sameer."

(Readers: I hate third party interference. That is why two is a couple and three is a crowd. Right now, she was a crowd between us)

"Okay then catch you later," I ended the conversation thinking that Priyanka will never let her speak. The words were few and the meeting was short, but after that meet, I actually played '*Pehla Nasha*' song more than a dozen times.

The conversation reaped the seed of a relation known as friendship. I used my time to pass at library, but not with the purpose for which the library was made. When other people were found busy with business magazines Philip Kotler, etc I was found with film fares and technology outlooks. That day she too turned up with her friends. She seemed beautiful with that single piece she was wearing.

I said, 'Hi' but she didn't respond.

She ignored me going back to whatever she was doing on the far side of the desk.

I also showed myself busy with other stuff. It may be, because our relation needed some fertilizer to grow. Nevertheless, somebody had to make the first move. People waste their time thinking about who will say sorry or who will come forward. Under such circumstances, the outcome is always negative. It's because they value their Ego more than relationship.

"Hello... can I sit here," Jasmine asked.

While I was thinking of some different way to approach her, she turned out bold enough to talk. I just wondered, "Am I a kid or a stupid college boy who is acting so foolishly on every act of her?" "Man! Be a casual guy, this is what you are, and you have to be," I said to myself.

"I asked you something," she waved her hand for me to wake up from the stupid thoughts I was concentrating on.

"Ohh... Sorry, I completely forgot."

"There is much more in this library than watching these hot shots," she said pointing on the vast knowledge in the form of books all over the library.

"Even if I spend every minute of the rest of my life reading, I do not believe that I will ever manage to read 9 million words routed on the selves of this library."

"Nine million…?"

Yap! If there are 250 words or so on every page and each of those books are 300 pages, and there are twenty on a shelf and six shelves per book case, why are you pushing 9 million words inside this small brain of mine?

"Oh… my god. Can't you pause for a while?" I just saw you staring at the hot chick inside the magazine. You might pick something else.

"Aha! You were spying on me!" my lips widened.

"I have been spying on you since a very long time."

(Readers: Boss, Vivek was so correct but I did not trust his words. I was so stupid who never trusted his words. However, it matters least when the project is still under construction)

"What do you mean?" I asked as if I wanted only her to confess.

"Nothing just a little joke", she said brightly. "I've got to have some fun, you know."

"You are crazy," I whispered. "So you must be missing your family here?"

"Yes a bit. However, Priyanka and Unnati are funny. They never let me think about my family."

"Are you going to read all that, I asked looking at the huge pile of economics books'?" I feared that if she was studious, I had to speak about marshal's theories all the time whenever I met her.

"No, actually I brought all here for you to... "

"Hold... Wait!" I interfered breaking her conversation. "You brought those for me". Are you nuts? I am not going to read that all. Even my father did not read all these and neither my grand father. My mother is just fourth passed and that also by giving buttermilk as a bribe."

"Ah... butter milk?" she exclaimed.

"Ya during those days in village, it was considered the best bribe."

"At least listen to me what am I saying", she screamed as I kept the books aside.

"I know all the butter talks of girls. You want me to read the books and make you dictate notations. Listen madam, I am not amongst those *lustful* boys who will do your work. I just want to confess, that the five ball theory was not of marshal but it was somebody else. Please don't misunderstand me to be a studious guy. I do not know even "E" of economics.

"So... who knows here, that's why I came to you"

We've just become friends and you've even started availing benefits from me?"

"No, I did not mean that." she cried. I just wanted you to read...

"I know what you meant. I would love to spend my time running all over Edi to loose my kilos instead of reading those books"

"Shut uuuuup!" she shouted making a lion's roar. "Will you keep your mouth zipped"? You are disgusting. Do you know what you are speaking? Amongst those books, I wanted you to read the topics and select the best one for my study purpose which covers our syllabus. Actually, in 12th I selected business management in options of economics so I even don't know "E" of economics.

I was silent because I had no words after it. On the second meeting, itself I made a fool of myself. I expected this tirade to put an end to the litigation but to my surprise, she looked right at me cool and collected. "So what do you want from me", she said.

"How do you know that I want some thing? I smiled at her.

I will select under one condition... aha not one but two conditions," I said.

If you agree, I will give you the best book for economics. Not from all these, but a book I am carrying away from my B.B.A times. My hand written notes.

"If you wouldn't keep the conditions then also I would have listened to you." She said smiling.

"I want you to forgive me for the rubbish I spoke now."

"It's okay. I already did and what's the other one?" She asked making a naughty face.

"I want to share a coffee at the near by *Amul dairy* with you and that also at your expense."

"There was no need to specify who will pay the expenses. *Kanjus (miser)* people like you have spoiled the name of Marwadi's."

"No, it's not like that. If I will pay, people will think I am taking you for a date," I said browsing the pages of her selected books.

"So, won't people think the same if it happens the reverse with me?"

"Why do girls ask a lot of questions?" You are all the same. You are paying that's it so that next time I can take you again to repay the favor," I smiled showing my high quotient for intelligence.

"Very smart. But I don't like coffee at all." she replied

"Ice cream will do." I continued

"Have a cough right now."

"So you mean the plan is canceled. Its okay if you don't come"

"Did you think I would really listen to you when you told me not to come?"

"Okay then, I will carry some *Bourn vita* from Mukeshji and you can have that mixed with milk," I said jokingly.

"Get out you two," a loud shout fell on our ears when we saw our librarian Ganpati sir standing in front of us pointing his uncut nailed finger towards the exit door for making so much noise.

I departed reminding her about the promise.

The next day we both went walking to the Amul station. I pointed a corner table finding the most comfortable spot. I ordered a double espresso for me and a chocolate croissant for her.

Sooner we involved ourselves with each other but then a buzz interrupted our conversation. I glanced down at the incoming number: no surprise there. I turned off the power button without bothering to take Vivek's call.

"Was that Vivek, she asked glancing back?"

"Yep...! I didn't disclose our meeting plans." I could not keep my phone switched off for long so I switched it on again and Vivek called again. She glanced up at me as the phone began to ring. "Speak up" she jerked her head indicating me to be normal.

"Hey buddy! I'm in a funeral. Not in a position to converse so call you soon," I hung up the phone and crossed my arms, looking at Jasmine.

"You lied to your friends," she gave me a measured look.

I struggled for a moment to escape from her weird look. "Yep, I did as I had no other option. Sometimes you have to hide the pastry to get all the pleasure alone." I answered.

"So I am the pastry for you now," she said.

"Chocolate truffle, I love that one. It makes my mouth watery." I giggled. A blush occupied her cheeks too.

"I also love chocolate truffle, it makes my mouth watery too," Vivek said from behind who came along with Ritesh & Rajesh dashing into our conversation at the Amul station.

"How come you guys here?" I asked feeling embarrassed.

"When I found Jasmine missing inside the campus, I went to Priyanka to ask about her", Vivek said snatching my coffee."

It's your bad luck dude as she pretended to be a daughter of Lt. 'King Abhinavsh Chandra' who was known for his truthfulness and told me about your destination."

I looked so uneasy when the romantic mood turned into a hunching crowd. I could not ask those people to get out nor could I scold Jasmine for telling Priyanka about the date. Finally, Jasmine ended up paying the entire bill for all the five of us.

When you tend to organize yourself, you become unorganized day-by-day. That is what I found in my self after a few days. Changes are good but what changed me was disgusting.

I couldn't feel a reason for such drastic change in my organized life into a *late latif's!* My room became a sea of dirty clothes and magazines left over junk.

After thinking on the issue, I gradually found that when everybody used to sleep I would be busy writing beautiful words for that mountain girl I just met. Was it love? Was it lust? May be a kind above all those?

I searched through the books and leafed through the cards for the words that I could convey but nothing better than this could come out from heart.

"In the silence of this mid night can u hear the whispering sound coming from my direction through the breeze, just want to wish u 'good night', hope u feel the care that flows with it. Lv C."

Even in the dark, I could see the shine of her eyes. I forwarded the above message to her at 3:45am. Nights are always long for people those who dream with open eyes and when it comes to daytime, they are found lying on their bed.

I finally discovered that she was special.

After play hunger started its act with rats dancing inside our stomach. The dinner was heavy. We guys got nothing to do so we made a step forwards towards the girl's gang. They invited us with open arms as if they might hug us after all. They chit-chat was general. Between the conversations joined, the hot and spicy *Anastha Singh aka 'Kattu'* what people use to call her? Words are not enough to speak about her. She was amongst the beauties in our college reflecting totally the *Dilli wala* attitude.

Now, what's next? "Any plans to digest the food?" A couple of friends placed an idea in front of the group to explore Edi.

The couple of friends were none other than Vivek, Vishal, Ritesh and Rajesh.

The idea was good but something fishy was going on in Vivek's mind, which was beyond my understanding. I signaled to come with me at the boy's hostel and started moving.

On asking what it was, all about he said, "With the idea to explore Edi we will take the whole group to different places where you can get some quality time to spend with her. As we reach the roof top hold her hand indicating her to stop. If she does you hit the jackpot".

I was silent. Seeing my silence, he was scared.

"If you didn't like, leave it, after all it was just an idea." he replied on seeing a mixed impression from my side.

"And what if she doesn't", I asked.

"If you cannot take out Ghee from a straight finger, why not try again by bending it."

A nasty grin etched over his face prompting his last words which forced my mind to proceed the other way.

"How can you think so much with your dirty mind"? I questioned him.

He stared at me with expectations as if I was going to do a great job. He was a guru. Not that guru of sex but simply a genius guru. His ideas, his speech, his words, and dialogues were simply amazing, encouraging me to move ahead with his thoughts.

Everything was going as we had decided. Firstly, we started with a casual walk at the campus and other places but then, Vivek's dirty mind started to gear up.

"Follow me, please!" Vivek's voice echoed. Ritesh and I moved closer as our group members huddled around.

We started moving towards the restricted areas where we were not supposed to go.

"Wow! That's awesome." I said.

"This is fun," Vivek whispered. However, I noticed he was clinging very close to me. As if, he wanted to say something. May be another freaky thought.

"Owe!" Ritesh screamed. "What was that"!

"What happened"? The girl gang asked curiously.

(Readers: why do girls being so curious to know the story behind an unusual act. All blames to Ekta kapoor.)

"Something passed over my foot. Might be a snake," he let out a startled gasp.

"Snake... are you crazy! Where is it?" Priyanka turned as white as a ghost. "I have seen big scary scenes like this in movies and comic books. I never thought that I will experience the same." Her voice trembled.

Priyanka really didn't like scary things – especially when they were real.

"Guys! There are a lot more things here. Not only snakes but apes, dears peacocks, and neelgais as a part of this jungle," Rajesh said. "That's why these areas are restricted for students."

Some of the group members laughed at Priyanka's joke but Vivek and I exchanged solemn glances. Staring at the dark jungle I pictured some one, standing apart, peeping at us. I asked myself, who was he.

I rushed to check out the person behind the bushes. His eyes glowed out from the shadow.

"What are you searching buddy?" Vivek asked me. We stopped glancing towards the dark shadow.

I poked Vivek. "See the man over there? The one in the black. Is he in our college?"

He scanned them and then looked at me right in the eye. "I have never seen him before," he whispered back. I doubt if it's human.

"He is weird but why is he staring at us?" for a moment silence prevailed between the two but then it turned to scream, when we actually found that the picture wasn't human anymore. It was a wild animal coming furiously towards us. We ran in fear opposite to the dark image.

I was feeling as if each leg felt heavy like a pound.

Oh come on yaar! Where have you got lost? Can't you move fast? Is there anything wrong? Why you are breathing so heavily? Ritesh threw a series of question. They seemed endless, like a series of darts thrown, so fast I cannot feel they sting anymore.

"Hmmm...Nothing," I said and started moving with the crowd. My eyes were still looking there trying to find the question mark, which I saw a few minutes ago.

"I advice everybody to take steps with open eyes," a whisper came out from Jasmine's mouth who was silently walking. The whisper was a bit loud as if wanting me to know her presence.

The place was dark and I could feel the cold sensation within me. While everybody was gossiping, I was simply silent; walking questioning myself, "Was I doing right?" Making plans for things not at all in my dictionary?

"Was I searching a friend in that pretty girl?" I asked myself

I thought to speak to Vivek that I wasn't in love as he had that wrong impression. I was totally confused to decide upon my feelings for Jasmine. I shook my head hard, as if trying to avoid the strange, troubling thought going inside my mind.

"What man! Why are you on the side? Silence doesn't suit you!" Ritesh said putting his hand on my shoulder.

"It's too dark." I complained, turning back to him.

Now say how is your Bhabhi looking?"

For a moment, I was confused hearing whose Bhabhi he was taking about, his or mine. My expressions were weirder like a scare crow.

"*Priyanka yaar who else?* See, how beautiful she looks!" something couldn't even stop him from becoming Priyanka Mehta's fan.

"We are going to climb the ladder. As you see, the ladder is narrow we will have to go single file. Please watch your steps." He grooved.

Ritesh and I were at the end of the line. The air grew colder as we made our way ahead. A heavy chill seemed to rise up the stairs with me.

"So many feet have climbed this ladder," I said to Ritesh looking at the beer bottles lying over the floor. After climbing for what seemed like hours, we stopped on a landing.

When we finally reached the rooftop all sat in a circle for a casual chic - chat.

When Vivek discovered that, there was no conversation between Jasmine & me, then he thought to 'bend his finger'. He placed the idea to play truth and dare.

Let me tell you that it is the worst game I have ever played in which nobody has guts to dare and most of the time the person is lying even while choosing truth as an option. We started with some typical Desi questions to know about each one's personal lives, but the thing, which made the game interesting, was a question raised by Unnati.

She asked everybody to open up and speak about his/her first crush at Edi. Hearing the question, I remained calm. I just felt like kicking Vivek.

I didn't want to cheat Jasmine with that stupid game. The question was passing by and I was ready with the answer. The words were revolving in my mind.

Finally, when it was my turn I was confused. Everybody was waiting to hear those words from my voice.

"She remind me of a flower pretty inside and outside, a reason why people smile everyday, a gift to all. She reminds me of a chocolate luscious and sweet, some people can turn into crises. She reminds me of a teddy cute and huggable; some people feel comfortable with, special to all. She reminds me of a balloon happy and bouncy; some people can have fun with, enjoyed by all. She reminds me of a lot of things but nothing can be compared to a real person, a friend I can look upon, cherished by me… me …. & only me. "Jasmine, she is the one" and there was a huge round of applause. My words had no control over my mind and so I could only realize the thing that has happened after I have said everything to her.

"So Jasmine any thing to his words?" Vivek asked projecting the real aim of – *The inside Story*.

"He is just a friend nothing else" she said. "I truly respect whatever he said because he is a nice guy. And I trust him he will always be there for me. I feel special now because he made me feel that"

I was listening to her words carefully and discovered that the things that Vivek and Vishal used to say were something kind of a *Grapewine that means half-truth.* They had forcefully developed a meaning out of nothing. She was looking at me but then I thought to proceed with no more assumptions to be made anymore.

After that serious interaction, it was now *Gaurav khadiwala* urff khadi's turn to say something. I thought, I was the one who is in everybody's talk but no I had a companion. Dear khadi was also having a crush on a girl at Edi with whom he never had a word. Before beginning, however, let me introduce this friend. He came straight away from Buranpur, Madhya Pradesh.

Simple and fair, with a nice body structure. If you want to know the secret behind it, it's simply khadi's love for water. Those three liters of water in the morning created a glow on his face and a pressure inside his stomach. Now lets find who was the lucky one with whom khadi had a crush on?

In his own words, "In life many girls came and many left, out of the many, few girls did like me but I wasn't interested. For the first time, I saw a girl extremely charming, good looking, beautiful, sexy and much more to be defined."

But... but and but... Later on, I discovered she was married!

She was none other than Payal Shah - Miss Hot@Edi who was married 15 months ago. When she came, our eyes couldn't stop staring at the charm."

A designer slim fit t-shirt with a low waist jeans, hair tied with a clip she entered in a catwalk style.

No proof of a married woman to be seen either on her neck or above forehead.

Few became fans, few started thinking about the hot chick and among the few was our Khadi.

"Bad luck! My love story ended before it started!" he said. Everybody laughed but I felt pity on innocent khadi.

"Hey, friends listen up" I thought to console him.

I have something to say on behalf of my neighbor. This is in relation to our second crush at Edi with Ms Shah. Second because the 1st one failed to make a mark (*Actually I was just making a fool out of me*). As a true friend philosopher and a devoted neighbor, if Ms Shah is listening (*looking towards the sky*) just accept the words and admire the care.

Everybody huddled closer to hear me better... I continued speaking solemnly.

Aap hamari mehfil mein yu aaye is tereh,
Shadi suda keh kar hazaro ka dil tod Gaye is tereh,
Kaun kambakth itna jaldi marna chata hai is duniya mein,
Yeh to aapke husn ke jalwe hai Jo paal pal marte hai is tereh.

I usually don't write 'Shairi' but that was something which came from heart. Everybody admired my creation and innocent khadi had nothing to express except blush. 'Mehfil' winded up with greetings. I was just moving ahead when I heard Jasmine saying "Good night Dev!"

"Good night Jass" I said with a low tone as if something was wrong. Was I feeling awkward because a girl said something, which was unexpected? May be because I was used to with the hype Vivek created and a single word of Jasmine made me fall from the ninth cloud! Whatever may be the consequences, I had to except the fact that Jasmine wasn't interested.

In Bhagwat Gita, lord Krishna has mentioned, "Things don't happen always when we are eager for it. Sometimes undesired things are fulfilled so easily giving you a series of happiness. Don't think and run for happiness, rather wait for it. One day it will surely come to you"

"What happened to your research?" I pushed Vivek.

"Don't worry dude! Friends can be great lovers but lovers can't always be good friends", he said. "Why don't you continue your love story by being friends?" he said rubbing his pointed beard with one hand.

I widened my eyes with an expressionless emotion.

When you commit a crime, it is but obvious that you gonna come in the eyes of law. While we people were discussing about the negative outcome from the project observed and planned related to Jasmine, there were lot more people who were also interested in this Garam Masala.

They were none other than the charming hunks and dudes of Edi.

They had already lived that life, which we had just started. Their journey to success as an entrepreneur, was about to begin for them. They were the 8th batch students, who recently joined us after enjoying their 40 days of internship period. For the first time in the history of Edi, we had two batches running simultaneously which added glamour to the *Mehfil* part. For three months, we were going to share a common hostel. They were going to end up with their semesters late and we people started quite early.

An experienced guy always acts as a leader, because for him dominance at the place or knowledge of the subject is quite strong. 'Dudes' what I use to call them believed that kids do ragging. They acted as the gurus who taught us the traditions of Edi. I could say that without those people, my book would have been incomplete. Like an elder brother who always feels powerful in front of the younger, they were also feeling the same self-importance in their broad chests discussing about their nine months glory.

Life was fun with those people.

Amongst all the seniors, ***Sinish, Boka, Abhishek, Sutta, Viral, Puneet, and Nilesh*** became the most happening dudes because everybody had their own individual story to narrate. Their experiences were mind blowing and you couldn't stop laughing upon hearing them.

When everybody was trying to be cool, ***Sinish*** was ultra cool. He had scored a century in the name of girl friends. During internship period for preparation of detailed project, he was celebrating his "28th Honeymoon" with his new Russian girlfriend in Kerala. He was a happening dude who could do anything.

Virendra dhanwa urff ***Boka*** urff ***Viru pajji*** was one amongst many who made the "*Kanjus Marwadi*" name famous. In Bengali, *Boka* means mad and there was no doubt about him. He carried a classic mild packet all 365 days in his wardrobe but every time one saw him, he was found begging a cigarette. He had done nothing except eating and shitting at Edi. This fun loving guy was always in talks for his deeds. It was research management exam for the 2nd semester.

Though he was a resident, then also he didn't turn up for the exam even.

While others were in computer lab giving the examination, he was busy downloading a porno.

Prof Yagnik the faculty in charge got a buzz from his main terminal that an X-rated site has been caught surfing from a girl's ID.

Poor Virendra didn't knew that the girl was present at the lab and it was he found absent amongst the 52. It was clear later on that greatest human personality also known as *Virendra* has bunked the second term research management exam and was caught downloading a porno in the middle of office hours and that to from a girl's ID. The professor caught him red handed in room no.37.

When asked about his absence and the porno scandal, he replied, "Sir I am extremely sorry for what I have done but I have story behind it."

I wanted to download some wallpapers so I searched on Google but as there was no distinguish made for good and dirty wallpapers a list scrolled in front of my eyes.

Being a typical human being, I listened to my lusty mind. I had a few more clicks and a notice blinked:

If you are above 18, please enter.

I calculated my age and found myself eligible so I had a few more clicks. Here also I played the role of that typical human being. Later part you know sir I took utmost advantage of the free benefits.

"I am sorry, sir, but all of that was absolutely free."

His words were making ***Yagnik sir*** laugh, but somehow he displayed seriousness and scolded him by giving a 'D' grade in the exam.

Abhishek urff ***Guru Bhai*** attempted in 19 re-exams out of 28 held at Edi during the whole year just for his friends. For every re-exam, he paid 500 rupees accumulating 9000 bucks. Apart from fees, he was the highest payer to Edi as income from other sources.

Why he did so is still a mystery to be disclosed later on.

Apart from *Guruji*, there was a person who was named ***Sutta***. I cannot remember his full real name because he had actually lost his identity with each puff of smoke he took inside. He needed two packets of wills classic everyday. His chain-smoking attitude made him suffer a lot. The situation was such later on that he couldn't even shit without a cigarette. His mouth and clothes use to send out a stink every time he entered classroom. However, all was well there at Edi.

Puneet, Nilesh, Yogi, and Viral were amongst the people who got two pleasures to satisfy their zest – drinking and gambling. While stock market trading was all time high in the morning hours, they also started "***37 China Town***" a gambling zone at Edi. During night hours, while others were busy with their assignments these four would be found searching people who would be ready to play '*Teen Patti*' with them.

Do you want to know the best definition of a rumor?

Rumor is when a series of Masalas are added by different people convenient as per their taste to a particular thing to make it spicier.

The dudes also came to know something spicy out of nothing. They heard that in the very first month, a boy named Dev has trapped one of the most beautiful girls at Edi and their scene was going very well. With these ill thoughts, they met me for the first time and started telling me about certain things that a couple should know, in order to have safe sex.

"Haven't your father made you learn about the self control stuff!"

Sinish came to see me with a gang of boys.

"Guys, I don't know what you are talking about. You are mistaken," I said.

"Mother fucker! Are you thinking we are fools? At least you would have caught hold of Jasmine after 3 months," Viru replied.

I decided to talk in their own language, which they could understand easily.

"When you guys are masters, there should also be someone from our side in the competition," I said looking into Sinish eyes.

"You are a new player dude, first develop your knowledge from base," Puneet interrupted, passing on the cigarette.

"Knowledge base?" I questioned with a dumb expression.

A list of *Khopchas* were placed in front of me to have secret sex and everybody started discussing about the pros and cons of each one. I was silent while listening to those fruitful advices from the gurus. After all, they were just passing their knowledge to the juniors.

Life was going good enough, so answering to rumors were not a difficult question for me. You feel special when there is some one who cares about you. Jasmine respected my words and wanted me to be a good buddy. Our togetherness in class, in the hostel, at mess and various different places was not only developing our relationship but also was creating false thoughts in other's minds. My behavior and acts were some kind of a public entertainment package for them. However, they had no hidden meaning, but people around came out with new meanings from it in the form of rumors. I neglected the issues, as I was least bothered but on the contrary what about jasmine?

I tried not to think about her but I could not force her out of my mind.

Her nature, so understood that when she got a buzz from me at four in the morning automatically she would calculate my position at nine. Most of the time, I could be found on bed itself. My breakfast plate would be ready, kept on the dinning table with a bread toast and some other eatables. Milk always occupied the menu because she believed that tea is harmful.

Somebody has rightly observed, "When night ends at four o'clock in the morning, something is going wrong." There started my unorganized life. I did not know why, but whenever I got up from bed it was something passed nine.

When Classes started at 9:45, it was very difficult to plan and manage as to which things to be given first priority. Brush your teeth, go for shit, or have a cool bath or breakfast, which ended up at 9:30. Mostly the sessions went very hectic because of hunger pangs dancing in my stomach. Therefore, to facilitate myself the morning schedule was designed likewise.

9:20: break fast for 10 minutes so whatever I could swallow, I did in those 10 min.

9:30: brush, and then have a shit for stomach relief.

If, 5 min remained I could have a bath with soap,

If, 2 min remained: just a water bath and

If the time was up for class, I used to have my 3rd degree treatment.

Mini shower! Is what I use to call was that barber's spraying bottle. A few sprinkles on head and a bit on face made me look fresh. Which ever option I opted after nine-thirty the result ended in ten min late for lectures. The professor had now got it all mugged up, words to be fired on me. However, that seems ridiculous but that became my life style. Body demanded clothes change twice a day because the

Deo effect vanished every six hours. That was a pathetic unorganized life I had started to live, and yes, indeed it was adventurous.

"Hi Mukeshji, what time is it?" I asked in a hurry.

"You are again late, the breakfast is over," he said looking at me.

"Oh, shit! Can you give me a single piece of bread....? Please!" I begged stretching the word please so that it looks pitiable and when there wasn't anybody, my prestige was still safe.

"Sorry dude, better luck next time, the breakfast is over." Mukeshji replied

"Okay then make something good for lunch," I said and started to move.

"Hey, Dev wait, here is your plate", Keshav shouted from behind. He was one of the staff members in mess.

"Oh thank god, I didn't think you will listen to me so fast," I said looking up.

"Don't thank him; rather thank Jasmine who left a plate for you. Here is a message she has left behind."

I read the message, *"Its study time so I am going. Here is your breakfast so gulp the food and shit in the commode. Do not come near me without taking a bath."*

It was a Monday morning. After a sound weekend, we started off with new freshness in our eyes. Prof. Siddhiqui gave us a new assignment to be finished by next day. A group assignment of four has to come up with the power point presentation on the topic, "Entrepreneurs who acted as a true leader of the nation." After the lecture, Jasmine and I united as a group including Rajesh and Abhinav who were left all alone as nobody wanted to take the dumbest in their group.

"So, on which entrepreneur we are going to prepare our assignment?" Rajesh questioned.

"*Dhiru Bhai Ambani* or may be *Rattan Tata*", Jasmine answered giving an option. "After all, they have their own success stories giving a boost to the others."

"Whatever you people plan, just tell us 5 minutes prior the lecture!" Rajesh and Abhinav left laughing at their own joke.

Jasmine was suffering from fever that day so I told her to rest and took the charge of assignment. I promised to see her next day morning 2 hours prior with a mind-blowing presentation.

That night Sinish forced me to join him for a DJ party. I thought to finish the presentation after returning from the party.

It was four am when we all returned. I was very tired, but I had to finish my work.

It's a fact that whenever we tend to think of sleeping for a few minutes it grabs a couple of hours from our schedule. The first lecture started but I was in my room, still sleeping.

Jasmine called me at my room to check. I was still in deep sleep. In the next lecture the presentation started. The Prof asked her about the group members. She thought to check where I was. On arrival inside my room, she was shocked to see us sleeping. It was heights and she lost her temper. She took a broom and hit me on my ass.

"Ouuucchhhh! Who is there?" I woke up in pain rubbing the wound.

"It's me your mother, do you remember?" Jasmine said. For a second she actually looked like my mother.

"Please don't beat him after all, he has the presentation", Rajesh exclaimed.

"Presentation.... (Pause) ohh shit... The Presentation! How can I forget that?

"Don't tell me you haven't prepared?" Jasmine looked at me furious. I had no answer for her.

"No honey... I have the presentation. Just give me 10 min to get ready". Five minutes passed and I still didn't knew how to make her understand that I do not have any presentation with me.

"She will not have a word with me the whole semester if she discovers about the DJ party being enjoyed in the name of assignment." I got a chill with wind chocking thinking about the disaster. While bathing I was thinking about how to get a PPT ready in 5 minutes. I took a deep breathe and released it. I did it 3 to 4 times to lessen the pressure inside my mind.

Suddenly I remembered Baba Ramdev – THE YOG GURU.

I developed a thought to present him as a social entrepreneur who has brought a radical change in the society in the name of yoga.

. I immediately came out of the bathroom and started working on my laptop. I logged on to Google and collected data on him. I also included a video of Baba Ramdev's yoga as a part of my presentation, which Rajesh use to practice with every morning. I called everybody for a last minute revision and distributed each one a part of the presentation.

After a few minutes when our turn came, I played the video. However, it was funny but the idea of social entrepreneurship was unique. Abhinav made his ass comfortable sitting on the professor's desk to demonstrate *Kapal Bhati and Bhastrika Pranayam* as a part of the presentation.

After the presentation, Jasmine was still angry on me. It was my fault to take the assignment lightly.

"I know what you are thinking" she interrupted, although I haven't said a word out loud. She lifted my hand and kissed the knuckles.

I apologized in front of the class admitting my mistake to Jasmine. However, people around us were making some other meaning of this relationship. It was not only difficult for me to explain things and clear their dirty mind but my acts were so that they made a different interpretation about me in their mind.

Next day somebody buzzed into the lives of every individual in the form of an email. Who was he was a question for everybody but he was well known as Mirchi Seth. The sender of this email was unknown but he was a genius guy who kept record of every student at Edi. He acted as an anchor of the *Poll Khol* program.

It read something like this:

Hi friends...

Here is the first Edition of Garam Masala... Hope u enjoy it...

MIRCHI MAILS

TUjHE mIRChI LAgEE TO MeiN KyA KarUN

(If you caught the chili, what should I do?)

Hi dudes and the so called babes of the 9th batch

This is Mirchi Seth presenting you the secrets behind the hidden cameras. I am there with Mirchi updates hope you like it.

Lover boy Dev has applied all the tactics to trap Ms charming Jasmine but finally ended up with a friendship certificate.

"It simply suggests touch me not".

Our Neta from Jodhpur Abhinav has started reading English novels so that he can get some few words to speak up in class.

Ronak Modi the poor guy recently lost 75000 in stock market *Satta*. The market fell when he was shiting in a commode. Mirchi Seth is contacting limca book records for the most expensive shit done in the world.

Miss Jasmine seems like a poker faced girl. If she is swinging around with our lover boy Dev, why is she eager to have a ball dance with the handsome hunk Chirayu? Dev finally has a competitor now.

The animal from Ranchi, Aniket has lost all his four underwear's. These days he is moving with just his pants on. "A price of 101 rupees is being announced on each underwear. Whoever finds can hand over the material and take away the price from Aniket." After all the underwear costs him more than the prize money.

While Apurva acted as a true brother to his sisters, his friends thought to apply the fundamentals and hang around with girls in the name of sister's hood. Lipika an eyewitness of the scandal has blamed Ashish of kissing his committed sister in one of the corner.

A few days ago, there was a fight between Ritesh and Shiven in the name of Priyanka. They were fighting for the ownership as if she was a public property. Now it's all upon her to conduct a *"Choosing the right groom competition"* to catch hold of the right guy.

There was a *"Daru gatkao"* competition between Sid and Ajay. Sid the fatso guy… who weighted 130 kg if he weighted a kg more, he would die of heart failure in his bed won the game after gulping 750ml of neat whiskey. However later on he fell on the floor unconscious demanding 10 people to lift the 130-kilo man from the lawn to his room.

Anna - the south Indian guy was found rubbing on his *Lungi* in the name of Ms hot at Edi. He was caught red handed when a couple of friends switched on his lights and caught him nude.

Anastha was found buying cigarettes from the tea vendor Sillu, so that she could puff in her room hiding the fact. Mirchi Seth is looking all over, so Anastha be caution.

Vanshi is a secured girl between the five musketeers Vivek, Vishal, Ritesh, Rajesh and Dev is moving tension free as she has body guards all around.

Sameer Patel and his puppy daughter Simran are living in peace now after the public feed him from back by bursting a bomb under his ass.

Ankul who is a resident student always stays apart from the hostel and has started living else where because of hygiene problems.

Mirchi mails are just created for fun. It does not intend to harm anyone. Mirchi Seth has high regards for everyone. No hard feelings.

U can always write back to me ... For any suggestion ... Best effort will be made to include your suggestion.

Mirchi Seth created havoc among girls after disclosing the facts.

The situation was so embarrassing not only for me but also for all those who became a victim. He was present everywhere. A fear was in everybody's mind that someone might be watching every time they did something wrong

Jasmine was sitting silent because she was also a victim. However when I read the mail again, I found many point raised by him seemed true.

If that was a fact then was the link up of Chirayu and Jasmine true?

I was looking at her with deep thought. She was sitting apart from me with hair open, wearing an orange *'Salwar kameez'*. She was looking so pretty that I could not move my eyes off her. Suddenly she started tying her hairs with a clip. I did not like it and not even the hairstyle.

I messaged her in the class itself, "You look pretty with open hair don't mess with them".

She had a habit to check her cell phone in class after every 30 minutes. A few minutes after reading the message, she clutched the clip out and left her hairs open.

She looked at me and smiled.

Modi and Gaurang, who were sitting besides me, also saw her expression. I don't know how they managed to have a glimpse of the message I sent her.

They just needed a hint to make it into a rumor and discuss it in public. It compelled me to think when everybody was talking bullshit about her and me, how she might be feeling. I had no right to spoil her image like this. There was a meeting held after dinner again for no reason and I thought it was a good chance to say my words but before I could utter anything there was a scene created which again forced me to re-think.

"Hey buddy I cannot understand this girl Jasmine", Gaurang said attracting people's attention.

"What happened anything you wanna say." Ankul interrupted

giving a serious attention to the topic. *There started a hammering session for a relationship.*

Gaurang wanted that people should know about the other side of the story, which was hidden.

"When she is Dev's girl why does she send as many as 20 messages a day to Chirayu? He has even received some messages from her sent by Dev."

"Do you have any proof to justify you statement?" Shiven said.

Chirayu came up with his cell and the message, "In the silence of this mid night can u·here the whispering sound coming from my side through the breeze, just want to wish u good night, hope u feel the care that goes with it. Lv D".

Ankul grabbed the portable phone and handed it to me.

"This was the message sent by her at two am to Chirayu," Gaurang said.

I saw the message and was shocked to see the *lv D symbol.* It was my patent symbol, which was sent to him with the words forwarded ditto.

She had washed off its meaning and made the feeling as a mere forward. I felt that was pathetic.

However, later on I thought, "May be she also considered the message as a forward and sent it to Chirayu for no reason. It's stupid to blame her for such a small matter."

Whatever it was but I experienced rumor potential behind and so I decided to drop the topic. Even if Gaurang was right, what difference it would have made to me? After all, she was just a friend. It was her life and she could do whatever she liked. Nevertheless, such rumors about the relationship were still biting me from inside.

They use to call them selves SAGAR'C that can be simplified as **S**-hiven, **A**-nkul, **G**-aurang **A**-bhinav, **R**-onak, and **C**-hirayu. **their** authority to rule over issues made them not only political but an important part to this book. Without whom, Edi would have been incomplete and this book would have no worth and value. Sometimes negative sometimes positive, in different situations, they acted as a godfather.

Let us begin the story with the stories of all of them.

Ronak Modi was a man equipped with lots of contacts to make any kind of work easy. Legal work or may be illegal. From *Desi to Videshi*, purchase or sale, Gambling or stocks, everything was his passion. He came to Edi loosing 10 inches of waist and a handsome 45 kg weight loss giving his personality a new avtar. His contacts were his assets that made him the most popular entity. From legal issues to setting one he had everybody to do his work. Abhinav had rightly said; "If you got stuked up in Ahmedabad, contact to the help line number **09824546053 - Modi**." With Modi as a dominating member of SAGAR'C, Abhinav played an equivalent role.

Greet Abhinav Daga, known by Dagaji in Edi as "*Vande Matram*" and you would see a naughty grin on his face. Now what is the reason behind it? Is it his love for nation or the germs of Netagiri? His parents forced him to study in Edi because they were fed up with his acts and wanted him to do something meaningful. The germs of Netagiri made him a leader. His vocabulary was fantastic. In order to create an impression he grasped a few hi-Tec words from the daily newspaper. Through out the day, you would hear only those words in his conversation. Whenever he had to speak something, somewhere or the other he would change the topic in order to fit those words in his conversation. Amongst all "*Playing with technology*" was his favorite line.

With Modi and Abhinav, the two-Agrawal boys also occupied a special place in the dominating group. Gaurang and Chirayu were not cousins but simply roommates who came to Edi after living a lavish life. While Gaurang who had a political mind, and gave the group a different method to rule, Chirayu created a charm in the group with his personality.

Ankul and Shiven were silent ghosts. They never made them visible but played as active committee members. While Shiven got jolly nature like hitting every ball with a six Ankul seemed like a silent killer. It was unpredictable about him.

The next week too I got trapped inside SAGAR'C politics. Abhinav and Shiven made me sit between their chairs. After the session was over Abhinav again opened up the topic. He wanted Gaurang to prove his words taking my side. I was simply too blank to react on the situation. When there was nothing for her why these people were extracting something. Whatever may be the things, I was still silent. But Abhinav was eager to know what was going in that girl's mind.

"What should I do to prove you that she is not attracted towards Chirayu?" He asked.

I thought it was none of my business to interfere in Abhinav's talk. But then a thought came to my mind to check my friend. If she likes him then she would have told me first. I was her best friend. If she was hiding things from me I would not forgive her.

Jasmine was sitting in front. She looked the same pretty girl whom

I saw on the very first day. Her eyes, the elegant refined hands, her dress, the way she did her hair, her voice, her step, always produce the same impression on me of something new and extraordinary in my life. She was gathering her hair to be tied in a knot. I asked Abhinav to type a message for her from Chirayu's cell phone.

"You look pretty with open hair don't mess with them and attract my attention."

But, with two conditions to be kept in mind.

1. She should not know that I have told you people to message such and
2. Message only when I am sitting separately.

They messaged her keeping in mind the things I told. I was looking at her from a distance. I signaled Ankul to send the message. A few seconds after, Ankul nodded his head on receiving a delivery report.

For a few minutes, silence prevailed amongst all of us. Nobody could focus anything else except her. Twenty minutes passed and there was no reaction from her side. Everybody was waiting for her to act but all in vain, because she did not see the message. After some time she peeped into her mobile phone to check her calls.

I don't know what I expected to see.

"I think she read the message," Vivek murmured in my ears. Everybody was looking at her but she was not aware about the plan.

After reading, she again continued to concentrate on class. While I was preparing myself, suddenly she bent down and gently removed her clip making her hair open. I was looking at her and everybody was looking at me. Amongst those smiling faces, Gaurang was the happiest because he proved his words correct and then I had nothing to utter after that.

I felt as if I got a hammer smashing down everyone who seemed like a nail.

Later on in the evening, I met her. "Everybody is saying you are attracted towards Chirayu, is it so? If yes then you can share it with me," I asked.

Seeing her unresponsive made me realize that silence has a sound. She looked up at me assuming the question has been put to somebody else and then got startled when she realized I am talking to her.

"There is nothing like this. Every body is creating rumors." She replied looking at me. "Trust me it's not like, what you are thinking, she added."

She moved her hands to press my cheeks.

However, that was clear, she did not want to talk more about it and later on, we departed.

When you show people this sentence "*godisnow here*" 95%of the people would read as they are shown "god is no where" but I am among the 5% people who reads god is now here. In that situation when everybody made it clear she was not interested in me but Chirayu, I simply denied the fact by ignoring it.

But the trust factor was still biting me.

When you have a relationship, the first thing you search in your partner is trust. Whatever the relation might be, people search trustworthiness in an individual. I was also afraid of my trust being broken. We had a strong chemistry and if any third individual was sharing the scene, nobody would have liked it.

The next day we people got together. The topic of discussion was the same. They were screwing me with their words. Finally I decided to end this all.

"Friends! Enough of pranks. Let us take the issue to one side. I am completely screwed up with the girl because she is acting strangely nowadays. I assure you that there is nothing from my side for her."

"So you mean to say you are not in love with her?" Ankul asked.

"Are you out of your mind? Who said this to you guys?"

"We heard that you proposed to her and she said no to you," Modi interrupted.

"Rumors! They are all rumors. I was just attracted towards her beauty. Then I added that I want Chirayu to do a favor. If you can break this hard nut, I promise I will kick her out of my life." I left with an unwanted statement passed.

Misunderstandings play a bitter part in every one's life. It is the only curse, which spoils every relation. I didn't want to create any, so finally I had a word with Unnati about the matter to know facts. She too told me to perceive everything as a corrupt mind's thought. Her words again created a trustworthy image in my mind. The next day Jasmine wanted to see me.

"Unnati told me that you both met yesterday," Jasmine said.

"Yes, I had some doubts that needed to be cleared," I replied looking downwards.

"Look into my eyes and then speak. I want to read your mind", she urged.

"My mind is a basket of confused thoughts so don't peep inside", my tone went half of what she urged but then I busted like a bomb. "Just tell me your scene with Chirayu. I know I am not your boy friend but I want to know for several other reasons."

"You are stupid, why do you listen to them. He is a nice guy I just met but why you are asking me? Hold on! Are you being possessive?"

I smiled at her listening to her words.

"Don't tell me you are", she passed a nasty grin on my shy look. We departed after dinner with a thought set in mind that this topic should not be discussed anywhere else with friends.

It's not always true that love is blind but sometimes friendship is also blind. Despite friends showing me the truth I was acting like a dumb person who didn't wanted to see the bright side of sunlight. However, when I believed in the words "god is now here" god was exactly with me at that point of time.

After a lavish Sunday at home I came up late at Edi on Monday. Sinish one of the seniors came rushing when he saw Chirayu and Jasmine together going towards the library. Germs of naughtiness to explore something undiscovered were present in everybody's mind.

A group of 20 people including me went to find out the secret truth behind the walls of library. Slowly and steadily, the group spread searching for the two. While I was in one group, searching them on terrace the other group found them close in one of the *Khopchas* at computer lab.

"Silence guys, you don't get such a chance daily to watch a porno absolutely live," Sinish muttered.

On one side, the dudes were enjoying the scene and on the other side, the couple was unaware about the things happening around them.

Message was sent to the group which I was in, that they were caught kissing. I was shocked listening the word "kissing." I rushed to see but by the time I reached, the gang made a loud shout shocking he duo. It wasn't that I was volunteering; I just wanted to know the ust of that pretty lady with whom I clashed at the classroom.

Jasmine's eyes turned wide enough in fear when she saw that she was caught red handed. A mass group of twenty has seen her doing the act when she intended to hide it. She licked her lips- they were still caked with blood – and it made her look like a vampire.

After some time she went to her hostel room keeping her eyes down. The scene hammered me so hard that it broke the trust factor and instead created a guilty feeling about Jasmine.

Later on in the night, Gaurang explained "The thing which you told to be performed in 3 days, Chirayu has done in two day and now if you still don't trust my words you are a complete mamu."

I have no solution for it because you are mad about her and you do not want to accept the fact.

He compelled me to think that the girl is taking advantage of my simplicity. I wanted to know my importance in her eyes. I could not even face her under this situation. That night was going to be tough.

Although we have not spoken for hours, I know that she is every bit as awake as I was.

I couldn't stop my thoughts going on a negative track. Whatever was the thing, that girl didn't deserve my friendship anymore. The next day I woke up late. It was already 10 and I was late for the lecture. I couldn't even have my breakfast. Bath was a far too distant matter to be bothered with. In the class, there was a fun loving atmosphere as the faculty was late. Everybody was sharing words, making noise, laughing with friends. I kept the books on desk and sat silently. I couldn't find the reason for it but I was feeling uncomfortable.

Vivek called me up looking at my condition. "What happened, Sirji, you are looking weak today?"

"Didn't have bath and feeling sleepy too," I made a statement, acting lazy.

"Hey, what you are wearing. Your t-shirt is stinking. You are wearing this same one since last 4 days. Tell me is everything ok?" Vivek said being concerned

"I woke up late so missed breakfast. The laundry boy comes early and I always miss him to give away my clothes for washing." I replied casually.

Listening to me he replied which made me feel even more depressed and worried, "why Jasmine didn't wake you up?" he said.

I missed the care, which she showed towards me. That kind of a mother's care from a friend meant a lot to me. Life explains many things through incidences. Every lesson is a gift that has to be taken into consideration. I made a mistake 2 years back by proposing to a girl whom my best friend loved. Though the girl was least interested in my friend but the mistake made was very costly. After that incident, she stopped conversation with me. I gave up the thing not because I was weak but I felt myself strong enough to let go of the matter, whatever it was.

After a series of happiness, there is always an environment of sadness. That is the rule of nature and life itself. I was moving away from the dark phase of life but people around me were just pushing me into it repeatedly. SAGAR'C gave a new meaning to our relation by declaring us a couple and later on Jasmine, a ditcher who went on with Chirayu. They were amongst those people who think that a girl and a boy can never be friends. SAGAR'C played a very negative role here by creating a very bad scene, which never existed. While I was nowhere in the imagined picture, I was titled "*Devdas.*"

I was taking this situation lightly, considering all as college fun, which mattered least, to me. I turned myself again into the same fun loving boy of Edi who could make anybody smile. I wanted things to settle showing that nothing has happened. But an incident happened which changed my life, changed everything, the joy the happiness and the good boy image. It was economics lecture in class and I was concentrating on what Prof. Minakshi pandey was teaching. Before the lecture began, I was busy searching for some important data on textile industry. I was so lost in my work that I forgot to have my lunch too. As it was already 2:30pm, I had to rush to class.

Out of the blue, I found that the graph on the black board was moving. I had a strange, tingly feeling that started at the back of my neck and ran all the way round my body.

I looked here and there to find the reason why things were moving. I could here the voices wavering around me. Something from inside was making me unconscious. I suddenly felt as if I could not breathe, as if my heart has stopped.

It felt so lumpy and hazard, so uncomfortable.

I felt as if I was in a dark closet, a frightening closet, I imagined the walls squeezing in, choking me, and smothering me.

My senses stopped responding and I fell on the desk.

What happened after that, I don't know. I just could see worried faces around me when I regained consciousness at the hospital near by. I don't know what happened to me but later on friends told that something was wrong with me.

I was admitted for 3 days for further checkups. Later on, I came to know from the doctors that I fainted due to high blood pressure. There was nothing to worry about. After being discharged, I was taken back home. My mother could not stop her tears, as it's the basic expressive nature of a caring mother. Four more days were over and now I was ready to pack my bags and set back to Edi. I got a warm welcome from my friends.

In the evening, all friends gathered discussing with me about the incident what actually had happened. I told them it was a minor unconsciousness and that was it and asked them not to worry so much.

Rajesh exclaimed listening to me. "Idiot, you are talking about worries. We thought as your mind is already screwed up these days, you might have eaten something." I could not even imagine what these people were talking about but one thing was clear. Everybody in college was giving this incidence unnecessary importance.

Firstly, there was nothing between us, and problems were breaking our relation largely and secondly this rumor. Under this situation when any body asked me how life was going, I had only one answer to all the questions.

"Life was fucked up completely."

Whatever was the scene I was hoping to get out of all these and have a *Bindas* life again? The next day Jasmine met me asking about my health and what happened to me suddenly.

"Is that true what people were talking about." she asked in a much tensed note as if something terrible has happened.

"Nothing," why?

"So what was it?" she asked me, again.

I was looking into her worried eyes. She looked down, her hair covered her face. May be there was some feeling left for me. Nevertheless, I wanted to stop all rumors. Even the scandal was running around my mind when she was found kissing.

"You have made a terrible mistake!" I screamed at her, my voice trembled with anger. "I don't know why I am here or how I got here!

But I am the wrong person you are messing up with!

I am not who you think I am! Whatever it was, Jasmine leave! You won't understand." I could not stop the chills that rolled down my back until entire body felt cold, numb, and tingly.

"You told me a lie and played with my emotions and then you forwarded my messages. My own hand written messages to a stranger. "I continued. " How could you do that to me?"

She was still silent. After all, she had nothing to say, or perhaps my words had zipped her lips.

She stepped back out of my shadow. I raised my hands to my chin and stared at her in horrified silence.

"It's time for us to be apart." I said, moving closer, with a whisper in her ears.

I could feel that I was losing her, but in order to stop the rumors I had to sacrifice our friendship.

"Can I say something?" she said. I realized too late that I have spoken out loud. I lean closer, because she didn't had enough in her right now to make words creep across the air between us. I answered. "Tell" - I want to make sure I have got it right.

Finally, she left with a note, which I could never forget in my life. The words were few but it contained everything what all she wanted to say.

With a low tone, she replied me "Dev, you never tried to understand things"

My throat closed like the shutter of a camera, so that any air could move through a tunnel as thin as a pin.

She wiped her eyes and looked at me. "You will realize." She said. "That you are the only friend I have got? I don't want to loose you Dev."

"That's not true", I immediately replied, but we both knew I was lying.

Then she left. Her words were vibrating loud in my ears. Though the duration of our friendship was very short but life seemed beautiful when she was with me. But then everything disappeared into thin air now, a *mystery, which can never be solved.*

Most of the time we think that friendship, feelings, care and relationship are special words which mean much, but actually in life they have no meaning because either they are governed by external forces which act as barriers in direct or an indirect way, or the selfish nature of man doesn't allow it to develop into spiritual things. My mind couldn't answer these questions that why does this happen.

Yeh hota hai to yeh aisa kyu hota hai ?
Woh hota hai to who aisa kyu hota hai ?
Zindgi baraf hai ho har koi jalta kyu hai ?
Pyar dawa hai to har koi Marta kyu hai ?
Har Kisi ke liye humdum hai to koi akila kyu hai ?
Sathi sabka hai to dil mein Dard dhakela kyu hai ?
Milne ke baad har koi bichadta kyu hai ?
Patthar pighalta hai to dil kathor retha kyu hai ?
Jaan jati hai to pyar zinda retha kyu hai ?

Zindgi jahnum hai to har koi shauk se jeeta kyu hai ?
Aasma mein rimjim rimjim Pani Barasta kyu hai ?
Barasta hai to har ek dil tarasta kyu hai ?
Yeh hota hai to yeh kyu hota hai ?
Woh hota hai to woh hota kyu hai?

ACT 3

Welcome to the dark side - Mehfil@Edi

The scandal left a sad mark on a beautiful story, with relations burnt into ashes. But, the joy wasn't over.

I could feel that joy was not in any of those moments spent with her. The joy was in me, which always acted as a boon. It was I, who created an environment of fun, love, and happiness and now it was time to create the same joy again.

28th August 2006,

I glanced at my watch. It was eleven-thirty five.

I saw the night sky, "Silent, calm and beautiful" but Puneet and I let out shouts of joy making it wild. But we did not care. A pale half moon slide out from behind wispy clouds.

Everybody was waiting for the clock to show 12.

After all, it was Ritesh's birthday. But, at the same time, people around had one more reason to have a blast.

Bad boy Puneet, the famous gambler of 37-china town won 17000 bucks in one game of "**Teen Patti**" with triple aces.

Therefore, when everybody of eighth batch was looking for a party from Puneet we people also had a reason to chill as well.

"So, dude! What's the menu for the party," I asked facing Puneet. "Are you ordering some good stuff to night? After all 17000 is a cool amount"? I continued.

"You will come to know about it soon," Viral interrupted.

"It's Ritesh's birthday today," I said and moved close to Puneet. Why don't you people join us? We'll have a blast together.

"That's a good idea," he nodded grimly. "Moreover, they will also come to know about our traditions," Puneet said.

"Wait let me call Shekhar Anna and arrange some stuff for the party." Puneet pushed the call button and began to speak.

"Who is he"? I murmured to develop my knowledge base about the unknown.

`Tring tring... tring tring....`

Anna: hello! Who's there!

Puneet: Billa No. 786, "JUNGLE SE BOL REHA HU"

Anna: Oh! Puneet sir, how are you? What are your demands today?

Puneet: "Panch kilo Bhandwal, Do khoka Agarbati, 7 SV aur 20 regular", kya samjhe. "NULLA MAL HONA MANGTA HAI."

Anna: Is there any sort of complaints till yet?

Puneet: ""TEL KA BHAW."

Anna: WOI - CH. Don't you think the demand is a bit high

Puneet: MANDIN MEIN BHEED HAI BHAI." I Am Coming

Anna: TANDOOR KE PICHE

Puneet: Ya there!

Anna: WHEN ARE YOU LEAVING?

Puneet: URGENT.

Puneet finally hangs up the phone, laughing at absolutely nothing. The conversation was weird. Seemed some sort of a code language.

"What were you talking with that person," I turned to him with a question on my lips carrying different vibes inside on looking at his unexpected attitude.

"Nothing it's not your matter of concern," he replied.

"At least I know you ordered the illegal stuff in this dry state," I laughed gleefully. "But you conversation was amazing".

"Billa no. 786" is our code and "Jungle" i.e. Edi is our destination. He ordered a "5-bottles of tequilas, a liter in each, "7-bottle" SV i.e. "Smirnoff vodka", 50 packets of classic regular i.e. a thousand cigarette butts and "20 beer cans" which we order regularly.

"Bull shit! Are you guys gonna drink that much", I asked in an excitement. "What were you asking – "*Tel Ka Bhaw*", I questioned again.

He was asking the rates of "Fuel vodka stupid," which was the same 650 bucks, Viral replied placing the cigarette butt between his lips.

"SV is cheap so we ordered that"'.

"You people are masters," I said widening my eyes with a lot of excitement inside.

"Welcome to the dark side – *"Mehfil@EDI"* Puneet said crossing his arms in pride.

Everybody moved around, arranging stuff for the party. It was still 15 minutes remaining when I checked my watch for the twentieth time. Actually, the partying fever caught my nerve. I moved my feet's with a thought to have bath. On arrival the movie was worth watching.

Tick... tik... Tik... 15 sec more to go... 10... 5.... 2....

The dudes had their own mantra of celebration – 'Jackass kicked off'. Soon the clock showed its three needles as one on twelve the party animals around busted with kicks and punches on Ritesh. Every donkey's leg in the chaos got up on Ritesh's ass to satisfy their zest.

It was fun but I was also feeling pity for Ritesh.

It was like a punishment in *Tihar jail* on his b'day instead of gifts and flowers.

He could not even walk.

Now you might be thinking that what a miserable birthday he experienced but nothing could be more miserable than the scene after this.

It was time to celebrate, but not for Ritesh.

He was going to cut a chocolate truffle and my mouth was getting watery just by looking at the delicious cake. It was very difficult to manage a piece.

"If"! It was my birthday, I imagined. At least I couldn't have missed the first bite. I lingered close to Ritesh and cheer him cutting the cake. As I was near him, the probability of getting a piece was more in favor of me.

If you want to know a live example of the saying "Future is uncertain" check this out. For pastry lovers like me, who are crazy about it, there was a lesson with a shocking moral.

As soon as I greeted Ritesh, inserting the first piece in his mouth the mob got violent. Sinish took the cake and smashed it on Ritesh's face. Viru pajji took advantage of the situation and smashed the remaining cake on me.

Soon there was cake on our hair, face, and hands, and everywhere except the mouth.

I took some cake from [illegible] face and licked.

However, my tongue found it yummy but my ears could hear some different and unmusical music playing in the background. *"Dil ke aarma aansuo mein beh gaye…."*

Now it was Ritesh's turn again.

He was made sit by the dudes and was told to remove his t-shirt after that the movie started.

Don't worry, friends, he was not compelled to strip in front of girls, but the seniors had their own commandments to be followed.

1st commandment: "Detergent brings whiteness and whiteness is a symbol of peace."

Nilesh applied detergent on Ritesh's hair that would him bring peace of mind. Ritesh didn't dare to run; after all he had to stay on with those people in hostel.

2nd commandment: "Tooth paste brings freshness."

Sinish applied toothpaste on his face which would bring freshness every morning.

3rd commandment: "No color discrimination"

Summit applied black kiwi shoe polish on his hands and face

4th commandment: "Hair on chest and body resembles masculine nature – The Macho Effect."

Ritesh had cleaned up his muscular chest, a thing the dudes didn't like, and so they applied shampoo on his body to make his hair grow fast.

5th commandment: "Fragrance of mud resembles the love for nation."

Viral covered him all with mud not leaving an inch.

6th commandment: "Eggs resembles healthy body and a sound mind."

Soon detergent was on Ritesh's hair, toothpaste on his face and shoe polish on his hands, shampoo and eggs on his body. And, mud on his armpits and waist.

But the seven commandments topped the deeds of all the six commandments. When all the seniors were applying irritating things on the birthday boy, they had a soft corner too for him.

7th commandment: "Water resembles neatness and cleanliness."

Buckets of water were splashed on him to clean up his body. After the bath, Ritesh and I went to get ready.

When we came, all were waiting for us holding the same chocolate truffle cake for celebration.

I feared if the seniors had planed the same thing again.

"I had already bathed twice and now I don't even have an extra underwear," I murmured to myself. The thought took me far from the chocolate truffle and I skipped this one too.

After the cake, cutting ceremony, the party started with *Desi dudes to Wideshi wine* to make a blast.

"Liquor and beer bottles" ordered by Puneet, "40 cola drinks,"

"Tanduri Murg" for the non-veggies and "Paneer Tikka Masala" with "Chips, Namkeen and Khahras" for the veggies occupied the party menu.

It could easily satisfy our tummy storehouse. I was looking at the scene, which I had never given thought before. May be it was a kind of celebration they did in their own style.

Twenty-five drinkers from the eighth batch took an active participation in the "HARDCORE DRINKERS RALLY."

The celebration started with the members of the rally standing on their knees in a circle with their mouth open facing towards the sky.

Their hands seemed to jammed at their back with handkerchief.

Puneet, standing in the center inaugurated the first bottle of vodka; after all, it was his party.

Within 10 sec, 100 ml of vodka was inside his body.

His hairs were wild and long, and fell in thick tangles behind the shoulders. He pushed them off his forehead. Tying them in a pony Puneet turned the bottle upside down pouring the divine water into the opened mouths of members standing on knees in that hard-core drinkers rally.

It all suddenly looked so unreal.

Everybody was looking at Puneet, but his hands and the flow couldn't be stopped.

He was moving round and round pouring in each one's mouth till the last drop got over and those who dodged him had spoiled cloths and vodka all over.

They were quite tough people to have neat liquor.

A foul odor rose up. The air was like a poison for the non-drinkers.

I was standing aside, looking at people and their madness for the taste of the 'divine water'.

They were surely going to love that moment coz DJ Parin was going to rock people with his beats. Considering the DJ system, this Edian had four speakers with woofers attached with two laptops, one of apple and another of lenovo, DJ software's fully loaded with his own music collection.

"Make Parin drunk and see the show. He plays the best music with this *hangover mood.*"

In such kind of local DJ parties, you won't be able to see any glamour. Guys were in shorts and Bermudas who were least bothered about girls standing in the party. For them the only matter of concern was the fun and the food. Out of them, ninety percent of the public was bathroom dancer.

Looking at the drunks and the way they were dancing the girl gang planned to move towards their hostel area. Music stopped and Sinish attracted the parties mood' as well as the skipping girls' attention with his speech.

"Friends, the girls are getting bored with your Desi immature moves."

"If your girls are really interested what kind of moves they wanna try with us," Yogi replied listening to Sinish.

"Some hippos or bangra, rock & roll or even a ball dance would do?" Tell your choice and Parin will play it."

While everybody was discussing all those bullshits, I closely watched Parin just to know the reason why he was known as the liquor king of Edi.

He has a zest for whiskey.

He decided to start a beer-manufacturing factory in Nasik and so he came to Edi with the same motive to gather more information as well as to give a shape to his business idea.

It is strange, but he was actually compared to Vijay Malya.

I was still looking at Parin.

He was silently sitting in a corner with glass in his hand lighting cigarette after cigarette to make his, senses work.

But from a closer view, there was something else going in his mind. I don't know what exactly it was but every sip of whiskey flowing through his mouth was concurring with his senses.

The smoke puffed from his cigarette was making his eyes dull as if it was revolving inside his mind. I thought he needed some rest. Like a sound sleep into his own dreams, with no noise around.

The party mood was getting wild.

Sahil a new player in the duke's hard-core rally had gulped half a bottle neat to show up his pride.

Woh kethe hai na "Jab pachti nai hai to peni nai chaiyeh"

It was the same case with Sahil. After gulping a large quantity, he was now trying to control the vodka inside his body. He moved here and there to digest it!

His condition was worth seeing but nobody gave a damn about taking care of him. He thought of diverting his mind, giving his body a rest.

He poured 45ml sprite to give a vodka glass look.

Then he moved towards Anchal, '*lighting a cigarette*'. He blows a smoke ring. May be he wanted to create an effect of his style statement on Anchal.

Sometimes, after the 12th peg goes down people do three things.

Type-1 people cry for their ex-girlfriend

Type-2 people talk rubbish about things, which have no meaning.

While, Type-3 people starts assuming persons like Anil Ambani as '*thief's*' who have no value in front of them. Because they think themselves on the ninth cloud so, they don't find any person superior to them.

"Sahil was Type-1 victim."

The conversation started with a few small talks. Later on, he started flirting around taking the advantage of the situation.

However, when he found that Anchal was not his cup of tea he thought to find a friend and started crying for his ex girl friend.

While he was talking suddenly, he gave everybody a shock.

The music was turned off and everybody gathered looking at Sahil and Anchal. He had no time to struggle. No time to try to break free. For him ground started to rumble.

I heard a groaning sound. A heavy slapping sound.

What he actually did was surprising as well as disgusting and deserved a slap from Anchal. If you people are thinking that he kissed her, you are on a wrong track.

"He literally puked the vodka on that innocent girl!"

There was puked vodka on her t-shirt. However, the matter of concern was, everybody came to know that she was not wearing a bra at that point of time.

In this situation, Sahil was lucky that he just got a slap.

I felt pity on the girl who experienced the worst nightmare. The girl gang left after the scene but the dukes were in naughty mood.

Suddenly Sinish pushed me towards the lawn.

The push was so hard that I didn't have a sec to read his mind. As soon as I was in the lawn.

Zappak...

Puneet, who was ready holding a bucket of water on the first floor, gave a splash targeting me.

He almost succeeded accomplishing his aim.

At that moment the only thing, I was worried about "*Aab chotha kachcha kaha se lau.*"

I was just thinking hcw much time it will take to dry my pants but then again a splash from Yogi and all the thoughts got washed with the splash.

I glanced at Vivek who was also planning the same prank to take revenge.

I saw a mischievous grin on his face.

"Ouch!" I declared. A horrified moan escaped my throat grabbing others attention.

I moved on to a corner and started to shout. All the dudes came to look what was wrong.

"Oww!" I screamed holding my leg.

Sinish...! Help! I can't get it off! It's hurting me! I cried in pain. I made them steady with my acts and then a splash from Vivek.

"I—I— I—" Sinish sputtered. His dark eyes glowed at me angrily. "I really thought you were hurt," he muttered. "Don't do that again, Dev," he said turning towards me. "I mean it."

"That's for getting me wet. Now we are even!" I stuck my tongue out at him. I know it wasn't a very mature of act.

With a swipe of one bucket, we succeeded in getting eight targets.

However, while everything was like fun, it was a bad day for Yogi's Nokia 3315. The phone died in that water splash accident. Instead of scolding Vivek, everybody thanked him. At least now, Yogi got to change his cell phone.

It was of that moment when Viral, Puneet, and Sinish came closer to me.

They came and lifted me for cheers.

At last, I found the best among friends with whom I could really enjoy the beauty of life. They knew how to laugh, share, and play pranks and now I was a part of them.

Viral who was on high after the vodka secession, now began to sprinkle the wet watery mud which had now formed on the ground.

"One splash from viral, another from Sinish, then me to Vivek and we did not spare the security guards too from our mischief."

The entire lawn of the hostel area became a grassless muddy land.

"The fragrance of mud was acting like a perfume in that hot atmosphere."

I checked my pants, and there was mud inside.

I was filled with mud in my ears, hair, body and mud was on each and every place, wherever your can imagine.

Sahil who did not even bother about Anchal's slap started drinking again to get back in that 'talli' mood. Over all this noise, there was one person who was silent, neat, and having pleasure in his own way.

Yes, it was DJ Parin who was safe; after all, he was making the mood of the party.

Now there was the song '***khai ke paan banaras wala***' on and the crowd dashed about with fantastic moves.

As time passed, the mud started an itching inside our pants.

Seventy people needed a bath and there were just 5 bathrooms.

I was thinking when my turn will come. These are the situations where an entrepreneur's mind works much faster than any other point of time. Give them the problem and they could bring a better solution but rather push them indeed and see they will come with the best solution..

"Why don't we attach a pipe," Puneet suggested.

But that was a flop idea. While some decent boys acquired the bathrooms, others thought to get into the queue. Among all, Viral was the one who was not comfortable with the bathrooms.

"What an idea," Viral shouted and started to show those Amitab Bachchan's moves.

Every.body standing there wanted him to speak but he was still enjoying his brilliant mover. Minds are like parachutes which works best when opened.

I think, in that situation he might have used 100% of his brains.

Then he spoke, "we always have been looking towards the beautiful fountain in our campus entrance,"

'So what's the issue behind it," Abhinav interrupted in between.

"*Lets declare it as beautiful one by feeling, it,*" he said and rushed towards the main entrance.

I think the dudes were not too happy with this thought.

They dashed to kick Viral's ass because the excellent opportunity was revealed at the time of their farewell days.

We rushed to the fountain and jumped without getting worried about the impurities. Yogi the best mechanic started the fountain flow.

Everybody had a great bath.

I took a step back and pulled my camera from my pocket. I raised the camera to my eye.

"Turn around Sinish," I said.

Sinish made a macho look twisting his right hand. I pressed the shutter release and snapped the picture.

Macho man Sinish gave more poses for a few clicks with just his shorts.

My stomach grumbled.

I suddenly realized that I was starving. The joy was enough to feel the hunger. After the bath, I don't know why psychological part of a human being needs something to eat.

As we were not apart from humans, we moved towards the cafeteria. We entered the mess kitchen and searched eatables like dogs do to inspect crime.

Yogi found some Biryani but that wasn't enough for those seventy staring at the plate.

"I think that is the same which was in lunch," I uttered.

Yogi simply passed out listening to my comment. He called me later on. I think he wanted to speak something to me but not in public. When I went to him, he spoke out.

"In Edi if you find bread don't go elsewhere to search butter for it. Have it and feel the pleasure because the dogs might have eaten your bread when you were in deep search."

It was miserable relating good friends as dogs but I changed my mind, as it was stupidity to doubt Yogi's experience.

We checked the whole mess just as a thief does for money but found nothing except Yogi's Biryani plate. Sinish planned to go at some dhaba outside but again a problem of transportation occurred.

My stomach rumbled again reminding me how hungry I was.

We moved towards the store. "It's locked. The door is locked yaar," Sinish bellowed.

We both lowered our shoulders and pushed the door with all our strength.

"Oh.... No!" the door did not budge, Viru spoke. "Open up," he shouted impatiently.

"One more try," I managed to choke out. Finally we succeeded in our intensions but then the integrants were kept in an almirah. The almirah had a long metal bar on the outside.

With all these confusions and hundreds of chattering grey mice dancing inside our stomach, I only thought of what I murmured.

"Why don't we guys break the storeroom's lock and have whatever we want."

Listening to my words, Rajesh got mad and scolded me a lot. He also warned me that I was his responsibility at Edi. But who could stop Viru pajji.

He brought an iron rod.

I do not know where he managed to get it from but somehow Virendra is always equipped with solutions. He turned towards the crowd and spoke loudly.

We all huddled closer to hear him better.

Viru continued speaking solemnly.

"On behalf of the members of the hard core rally I welcome the junior batch to commit the first EDI 'Kand' under our supervision.

When you have entered into a stage what actually we call it as illegal why don't we jump above the heights and cross the limits.

Friends this time you people have to make us proud and give a feel that after us you will continue the tradition of Edi.

A tradition followed by our seniors. We gave a new definition and now you brave hearts have to continue the era. We are here to eat drink and have pleasure....

"So come on and show us that breaking a damn lock and dashing into a store is just like a puppet show for you".

Everybody laughed looking at him. His speech was marvelous but he actually made a fuss out of himself. Nobody reacted to him. "Oh come on! Don't show me your dumb faces. You guys are *Cowards.*"

We knew that breaking into the almirah and stealing eatables was a flop idea.

The director could expel us all for the deed.

It suddenly started feeling cold. I had my hands shoved deep in my jeans pockets. I could not digest the word Coward.

Viru's words echoed in my ears. It annoyed me. I couldn't keep a straight face any longer. I turned back and gazed at the rod which Viru was holding.

I grabbed it away from him.

"Move back"! I jeered and banged the rod on the lock.

"Dev— leave," Rajesh cried in a shrill, startled voice. He tugged my arm but there was another bang and the doors to heaven were open for all.

His arms shot forward as if reaching for my safety. My brother's eyes were popping out of his head.

With a heavy sigh, I raised the rod towards Viru.

"Brother, if you still think we people are Cowards I feel that you have to think it over twice," I said in a trembling voice. My breath was heavy and full of excitement.

Those were my last words and then my friends carried me and swung me in cheers.

I came forward and told the dudes "We guys will continue the traditional era with a difference, a difference which will make you feel proud. I confessed.

Sinish wraps me in his arms; Rajesh caught himself between us like a gasp.

He took me inside the store and asked me what I will have. This time Sinish was the chef who was going to prepare some delicious mouth watering stuffs.

"What will you have, buddy?" Sinish said asking my choice. He pretended as if he was really going to make the food of my choice.

"Anything, which can be served in 10 min, would do," I said.

I gave that quick answer because when mice are dancing inside your stomach you don't have to listen to your heart. It is the mind who answers all the questions.

Nilesh picked up some eggs and a few bread packets to prepare his favorite *Andda Burji.*

The mess kitchen became house full with people starving for food. Everybody was told to leave until the guys in kitchen are done with it. We all went towards the lawn. We laid down on one another waiting for the food to be ready.

While Puneet was busy with bread toast and egg Burji, Sinish planned to give a vegetarian taste with his Maggie noodles. Yogi and viral couldn't manage to think over a dish to be prepared.

Finally, the duo planned to use up the fried Papads left over after the dinner. They started to garnish them with onions, capsicums and tomato's all over making *Masala Papad* the easiest of all.

The table was piled high with food – Noodles, Biryani, Burji, and Bread along with masala papads accompanying them.

The food was just strewn over the mess table for people to reach in and pull out what they wanted.

The feast was ready but the sufficiency was doubtful. The strong smell of Maggie noodles choked my nostrils. Donations were welcomed for eatables provided by moms with their extra caring nature. There was no plate system. We divided in three groups and the food was served.

Before we started to gulp in, Abhinav shouted and stood up.

It was 5 am in the morning and everybody was waiting to break into the feast. Exactly at this point of time when eyes were asking for rest, stomach was asking food, and the nose which couldn't stop breathing the smell came from Maggie, *"Mother fucker Abhinav wanted to give a vote of thanks speech"*.

"It was only yesterday when everybody ate noisily, talking loudly, laughing, and singing, taking long drinks from the crystal Tequila glasses, slapping the cups on the table top and toasting each other merrily."

Vodka was in the air. People were so crazy that they broke into the store for food.

Suddenly there was a slap on my ass while I was still dreaming about that crazy moment. I waked up swimming up from the dark to focus on his face. It was Abhinav the VANDE-MATRAM BOY with a good morning smile and a bad news.

"What the fuck man," I crawl out of my bed. "I was just going to break the storeroom's lock and there was food for the starving innocent people. You spoiled my mood, yaar."

Dreams are always sweet, as they have no harshness of reality.

Abhinav was angry with me because whatever I was talking got no meaning to him.

"Hey, buddy! Sorry to disturb you with your dreams but you actually broke the storeroom's lock yesterday night itself," he explained.

I silently stood up scratching my hair to recollect the incident and then there was a bang with a click from the door.

"Ohh shit! I broke the storeroom's lock," I shouted.

I was startled by the tense, sorrowful expression on his face. "I am so sorry to give you this bad news," he said,

"Huh? Bad news?" I whispered, moving closer to him.

"There is a panel of professors standing outside our hostel with Mukeshji, regarding the material stolen from college hostel. "They are frantically searching the thief, and that means us."

"This can't really be happening to me," I declared shaking my head.

"Yes you did and now they are going to fuck your ass for the crime," he muttered.

I took a step back, out from under his hand. I studied his face.

Was he joking? Was he crazy?

His eyes revealed only sadness. His expression remained solemn, too solemn to be joking.

"I think they are going to call the police because of the theft," Abhinav announced.

I felt a stab of fear in my chest. I kept glancing at Abhinav. I waited for my heart to stop pounding. I forced myself not to be dizzy, not to give into the terror that rose up over me.

As our two faces turned worried, another worried face joined us.

It was Rajesh who was making the situation more tensed with his typical dialogs.

"If you go to jail, I am not going to pay the bail money as I'm already getting short of it," He frightened me with his words.

"Okay, okay!" I replied impatiently.

I made a disgusting face. "Brother, you are such a wimp! You have a bad feeling about losing money.

I managed to keep him pretty calm, as I was a lot less wimpy than he was.

It was high time for the dudes as tension prevailed on all the Maggie lovers who dashed without thinking of the consequences.

"Lets go out, the professor is calling us." Vivek pleaded. His eyes twinkled merrily looking towards me.

"Will you confess your crime"? He asked. The question bounced through my mind as I scrambled down.

"No man... How can I under such a situation"? My cheeks were on fire; my heart started pounding. I felt like I did the time the principal caught me because I drew a sketch of my history teacher and her colossal butt in the margins of my class notebook

We were directed by the authorities to stand in a queue. Students of both the batches gathered with a simple question forced to their mind.

"Who dashed into the store and stole the eatables"? The Director demanded.

The answer was much more difficult than a CAT entrance question paper.

"I am not going to tolerate the scene. I will take care of the responsible person, being expelled from the college."

The sound boomed louder than thunder.

Rajesh and I froze in the middle of the floor. I could hear Rajesh's raspy breathing behind me.

"We will get out of it soon," I nodded looking at him giving an expression of confidence. I don't know why. It's not like shaking that would help fix the problem. But than also, I did to stop the sweat falling from his forehead.

"Do you give this in writing," he demanded nervously.

"That is strange," I uttered glancing at him.

"Do you give this in writing whatever you said," he repeated.

I hesitated. "I'm not sure," I told him in panic.

The frightening words from Prof Bakshi gave a jerk to everybody but the most miserable scene was "After each dialogue the dudes were looking at me with at a smile."

Everybody had an equal share, so why did I have the frightening feeling of being the accused. I wondered if I was thrown out of Edi what would happen.

"Angry dad, his fruitless job, early marriage, early kids .... Oh no!"

I was desperate to find a way to escape. At that moment, I remembered the golden words.

'Mumma said, "Whenever you get stuck up in a mess, remember two things. Stay calm and remember God he will surely help you".

May be some people don't believe this logic but at that point of time I had that as the only option left. I closed my eyes and took a deep breath.

I held my breath for a while and silently whispered in heart.

"Hey bhagwan aaj bacha le, if you promise to save me today, I promise not to repeat–AMEN."

When you wish for a toffee and you don't get it, please don't panic. Be silent and wait because God might have kept some temptations for you in the refrigerator.

The wish really worked out.

A friend, philosopher, and a guide, the threesome combo pack Prof Minakshi Pandey acted as a real guru at that situation.

She took all of us aside and politely asked, "Students, I know it's your work and I don't want to know the name who did it." The problem is everybody in the panel and Mukeshji is confused that the stealing was either from student's side or by the mess employees.

"Please tell me the truth so that I can handle the situation before it gets out of my hands."

It felt like a fist in my gut, now that its here and happening. I stepped forward. What I could possibly tell her?

Sinish interrupted, "Man, we tempted him to break in. It's not his fault alone." Everybody standing here had an equal share from the feast. If Dev is going to be punished, we want an equal share from his punishment too.

Yogi, who was in the mess committee, came forward to meet the professors with a note of apology.

Hello sir,

I, the active member of the mess committee admit that the offense was committed by us and all the resident students were a part of it. I apologize humbly for the deed and promise you not to perform it again. I personally apologize, Mukeshji for stealing the eatables and we are ready to pay the charges, whatever they may be. If the committee thinks that we still should be punished, we will respect you decision.

Anything in polite works. The sophisticated English used by him was so impressive that Mukeshji came forward and changed the environment with just his words.

"After all, these are our children, if they will not eat then who will enjoy the pleasure." He hugged Gaurang and forgave the charges.

Rajesh breathed a long sigh of relief. He clapped his hands together as if he was gearing up for a cricket match.

I also let out a long sigh. My heart was still pounding like a brass drum. But I felt a little better hearing Mukeshji words.

However, Mukeshji warned him at once that if he needs something he could ask the store keys and take. The last words brought smiles among the students.

The sky was getting clouded indicating the time was changing.

Love, friendship care, and fun were spreading not only among the students but also among people with different age groups.

Everybody was happy, making EDI a dream where life seemed beautiful.

As a movie has different phases, I also experienced many such phases at Edi. The fun and the food were a basic need but something, which was more important than all this entertainment was learning.

Studies were always a matter of concern apart from party stuff. It was our 1st semester and for the eighth batch students, the last one. I got involved in books leaving fun aside.

I do not understand that why students read lumpy books only when the fear of exams is revolving around.

If the fear was terminated, how many Newtons the country would have produced! Whatever may be, but we were here to study without fear.

Being in the seniors company, I was getting that bad boy's image.

The examinations began the next day. The 1st paper was Economics. But I was in no mood to study. As usual, I bunked the fourth lecture and got involved with Sinish and company for gossips.

After the evening classes, nobody turned to the volleyball court, however. Deep in books, with sleep in the eyes, was the common appearance of boys during midnight hours.

But where was I? At a road side restaurant on SG highway having delicious stuff, where else?

It was 2 am and we were munching like dinner for the second time.

"What to do for tomorrow's exam," I asked. "It's really a tough paper and Prof. Pandey has more expectations from me."

"So, why are you here, you should be studying?" Viral said.

"It's okay with me". I have done my specialization at graduation in this subject it is not a matter of concern for me but what about you guys? It's your final semester.

If any one of you fails then you would be screwed up completely." Puneet laughed at my innocence.

These people were much wicked than I had thought. Viral, the cleverest among all, gave me the MAGICAL ROD, meant especially for exams.

There was no need for it, but it was simply amazing.

"When you leave from here, do what I say," Viral started to speak in confidence.

Check out the course curriculum. Switch on you laptop and log on to Google.

Type each topic and copy the data from Wikipedia or from other websites.

Paste the data in a note pad. "Remember do not copy in word document or elsewhere but only in note pad."

I have my notes given by the professors! "Why a notepad? Anything special about it?" I asked. Every word of his was showing the wickedness of his mind.

"Ya, it's special," he replied.

"Actually, that file can be easily transferred to our mobile phones and we have all the answers.

Tomorrow when you go for the exam, please carry two mobile phones. One is to keep near the supervisor's desk and the other with the data between your legs below your scrotums.

"No one will find the secret behind your success," he laughed.

"Bull shit! You are such a bastard. What an idea! Sirji," I said being amazed by that corrupt mind's thought. "But why are you people not planning to do the same," I asked in a confused state of mind.

"There is no need dude," Puneet uttered. "Under the shadow of ***Guru Bhai*** none one of us will fail." The boy was a super hero for the dudes.

"While others were in examination hall, our Guruji would be found in one of the hostel room with 2 laptops, books, course material, data, answer sheets and 3 cell phones so that he can get the answers his cell phone and everybody could avail the benefit through a text message sent from guru."

The chemistry was solid and nobody at the staff had known knew a word about it. Even the girls, who didn't talk to him usually, began fluttering around him in exam time. This turned to be the reason behind his nineteen re-tests.

The next day I woke up at 9:30.

"Oh, shit"! I exclaimed as I opened my eyes looking at the lying books and notes left over.

The exam was going to start at 9:45 and till now; I haven't read a single word!

I washed my face.

With the water splash, the overconfidence too washed out. The last minute tension occupied my mind and I could not see any ray of hope.

Between the thoughts, my mobile buzzed and it was Jasmine with a best of luck message. I was tensed from the beginning and there was another thought arising.

Time was running like P.T.USHA.

I kept the cell aside and began to read. Suddenly I remembered the mastermind's words.

I took my laptop, opened wikipedia, and copied most of the data in a note pad file. Transferring the files into my n-gage phone I rushed to the examination hall.

It was already 10 and I was late as usual. When I entered the class, breaking the rhythm the supervisor was shocked to see me in boxer shorts.

In all that rush, I actually forgot to change clothes and have a bath. He ordered me to be dress well and come. I was already late and I did not want to lose more time. I rushed immediately, wore my cargo over the shorts, and came back again in a minute.

I took the supplement and began to write.

I read the first question and a naughty smile emerged on my face. With two, three and four my grin grew wider. As I completed reading my grin grew so hard think my face might splinter. Actually all the answers were in my cell phone. If I would have written the paper completely, I was sure to score A+.

The first question was very lengthy.

It was only thirty-five minutes past ten, and I asked for an extra supplement.

Every body was looking at me with a worried look, but I didn't bother to give an eye.

The supervisor came near me while I was writing to see if there were chits in my hand. However, after finding nothing he went away. I asked for the second supplement when all were writing in the main copy. Now the supervisor became more alert and he started to constantly stare at me as jasmine did.

I was still busy writing, giving an impression that I knew everything.

Nobody could see that there is a cell phone under my butts.

Despite of bunking lectures and roaming all through the night nobody had expected me to be doing so well.

The supervisor was in a very a strict mood now. I thought to hide the cell phone for a while and began to write. While I was writing, he suddenly stood beside me, peeping inside my paper.

The six-pocket cargo saved my life.

That's what they are made for, to hide things. The supervisor told me to get up and show me the paper.

Actually, he was searching for chits. As one cell phone was kept on the desk his thoughts didn't move that way.

The illusion was fantastic.

He checked my hands and then finally ended up with no clue.

"I am a sincere student," I said softly making an innocent face creating my impression on him.

After he left, I again took out the phone and began to cheat.

I wrote almost everything what was there in those note pad documents.

The supervisor was still confused about me. He moved here and there keeping an eye on me. When he came near...

"Sir, shall I stand to give you a perfect check-up," I asked giving him a trustworthy impression. "If you want to even remove my clothes, I won't hesitate."

"No, its okay, you better write the paper," the supervisor said.

"Please do not take me wrong, I am an intelligent student," I whispered again when he passed by. "Trust me! It's my specialized subject".

"Yes, your attendance in the economics lecture is showing you sincerity."

I have the list. 64% is a shame.

I know you are copying but somehow I am not getting the clue.

"Don't panic sir, I won't give you any." I said glazing around hiding the lie beneath my eyes.

"Now when you have written it completely why don't you utter the secret behind it?"

"I won't fail you but I am getting impatient to know, despite my tough supervision how could you cheat," the professor said showing his eagerness.

"Sirji! If I could not keep my secrets inside me how I could trust you to keep the same." I left the hall with a strange note. The supervisor was still under that illusion.

After all the 'Magical rod' worked but then I promised myself to study with sincerity in all the remaining exams.

The exams were over and everybody planned to enjoy the weekend together.

Our seniors threw a fresher party for all of us. But in the presence of management gurus and the professors the event remained of a kind in the funeral.

It was a flop fresher for them but not for us. We had another trip waiting towards Mount Abu. Ronak Modi arranged the trip using his list of contacts. The journey was exciting. Though Jasmine was in the bus but I never thought to give my attention.

Finally, I threw her out of my life.

The next day Mirchi Seth banged with an E-mail moving with his second episode of Garam Masala.

Hi friends...

Here is the second Edition of Garam Masala... Hope u enjoy it...

MIRCHI MAILS

TUjHE mIRChI LAgEE TO MeiN KyA KarUN

(If you caught the chili, what should I do?)

Hi Dudes and the so called babes of 9th batch

Mirchi Seth is back with Mirchi updates ... More than 95% readers wanted this whirlwind to continue so I am back for u.

Ready to start a new semester after sucked up exams....

"Our leader from Jodhpur, Abhinav celebrated the Vande Matram day with all devotion and love for India wearing everything in khadi including his under wear."

"Ronak Modi titled the 'Ghapla king' of Edi has resigned from organizing cultural event and fund raising activities as he felt really bad for being blamed of doing fraud in the Abu visit with the innocent batch mates".

"Miss Jasmine has finally cracked the hard nut". She was caught hunching and munching with the handsome hunk Chirayu. After knowing about the secret corners for love making our dear batch mates have finally started using them."

An eye witness has forwarded a sex tape of the recent *Jass khopcha kand* to Mirchi Seth. If readers want a copy for their personal leisure's they can get at a CP of 200 bucks.

"Ajay has no time for love as he spends all his time with books after Miss Rishita went back to her den leaving the institute."

"Miss Rishita left the institute, not because she did not have the guts to go on the stage and give the presentation but actually is our friend Ajay. He who had fucked her in dreams so many times that she has just become a bone poking sharp through the skin of her t-shirt."

"Miss Aditi left the institute as she was feeling lonely after Miss Rishita Gupta had left. Mirchi seth can understand how you are feeling Aditi "

Apurva went out of his way helping students for the computer practical. He was screwed by our lover boy Dev asking a series of question. They were brainstorming so much that he himself forgot the solutions ending up with a D grade in exam"

"Ritesh celebrated their birthdays where the friends danced all night in hangover."

"Unnati who was suffering from Jaundice, She did not have enough stamina to attend the classes. However, she had all stamina for dancing at fresher's and going out for movies and now she moves with her new cap on head like an Umpire, guiding the girl's gang".

"Shiven still spends all his weekends in Nasik. His excuse is work but actually it's not for work but with bar dancers making them strips at his hideout".

"The SAGAR'C had a wonderful time in the lap of nature, mount Abu."

Gaurang Agrawal took initiative of economic lecture for his dear batch mates but everything winded up with zero presence before the session began.

Ankul fasted for more than ten days, taking help of religion, thinking that he will lose some weight but at the end, he has gained more weight.

Priyanka now rides a Kinetic which is worse then a cycle, it a scooter just because it has an engine and can stop anywhere.

Mr. Rakshit gave a motivating lecture about the redundancy of books and a need for practical thinking. Later on it was found that it was only he who was inspired from the speech.

Payal turned "SIZE-ZERO" spending more time in girl's hostel than her home as her husband slapped her for buying extra short skirts to be worn in college. Mirchi Seth feels sorry for the clothes unworn.

"The south Indian gang is really missing you payal, hope you get time to shower your sex appeal towards them."

Abhinav and Neel went to Delhi to attend agro fair; they seem like serious dudes who are not like others who are thinking the course to be a paid holiday.

There are rumors that Ashish is seeing the Delhi girl Anastha, and has warned people to stay away from her.

Rajesh Jhawar is trying hard to turn happening with his new 'Gajini' look.

Fat soo Sid you is really missed by all of us. Please drop in sometime and thanks for the response to previous mail.

Vivak, Vishal, Vanshi the triangular series is moving through tough times.

"Dhaval is slowly learning English; he is now more confident and has cracked the OB case."

"Sameer Patel who dreams of becoming an accounts professor at EDI ... is slowly moving toward his dream with his family simran and kanta.

Mirchi mails are just created for fun.

It does not intend to harm anyone. Mirchi Seth has high regards for everyone. No hard feelings.

U can always write back to me ... For any suggestion ... Best effort will be made to include your suggestion.

"It is a rule from the Almighty."

'People and joy do not be with you for long.' I could not feel when days passed so fast and time came for the eighth batch students to disperse.

A notice was placed for PGDBEM students regarding the 8th Convocation to be held on 28th of June. In a very short period, they were going to move towards their respective places leaving everybody in illusion that they will come back.

However, this did not make the energy level of the dudes go down. They were tough and knew that the day was going to come. The enthusiasm to enjoy the last moment was much stronger than the feel of getting separated.

ACT 4

Dukes of unknown identity

The convocation dates moved like a derby horse running towards the finishing line. But spirit to rejoice hadn't faded inside the hearts of the dudes our seniors. They just lived today as if there is no tomorrow.

That laughter which they carried so high today was going to turn into memories tomorrow. I have seen them being like a tiger fighting for all odds; like a boxer, coming up swinging before the next punch can be thrown by fate.

I told myself "No matters what people say, I'm going to keep it cool spending my quality time with them". After all, who knows, when would their eyes catch this Humpty dumpy image again! I scheduled my time to get busy with those guys instead of attending boring, uninteresting lectures. The addiction which I was getting with Sinish and group gave a heavenly feel like sniffing cocaine. At no point of time I knew that this drug will result worse for me.

It has been rightly said, "A man is known by the company he keeps & the company, which I was keeping, was slowly getting me detached from my own batch mates.

14th September, 2006

It was a beautiful day. I was in no mood to get involved with the lecture going on in class. I joined Puneet, Viral, and Sinish. When I entered, they all were busy with the poker game. I took a picture of those guys.

I had no clue that it would be the last picture I would ever take.

"You people will never grow up. At least stop this stupid idiotic game when these are your last days here. Life is fun, look at the sky, cold and cloudy; like its going to rain. You life is going to change soon; you are going to be busy bugs like an ant. "Why don't you assholes throw these cards and do something meaningful?"

"Sla..ppppp". Sinish printed his five on my cheeks. They became red like strawberries. I have never seen him like this before. I wondered if my words ignited him but on the other hand, these were no such harsh words which will make Sinish do this.

He shouted and asked me to get out. I was annoyed by his reaction which seemed out of the blue.

While I was moving out, Puneet whispered, "Don't let this guy enter."

"What did you say," I whispered to Puneet.

"I said get out, don't you understand simple English. You know what you are? An ass hole, a simple mother fucker chewing gum who had stuck into our shoes" He looked like someone I did not recognize. But why was he speaking all this to me.

"What is your problem?" Sinish started the rubbish. "Why can't you place your ass somewhere else?" He was talking as if I were some kind of machine: a car with a faulty carburetor, a plane whose landing gear is stuck and you want to get rid of the thing or the situation as soon as possible.

Without an explanation, I got to my feet and moved out of the room.

The words were simply unexpected. I felt so bad that. I decided not to see those people ever in my life. The joy we experienced had no meaning because I was a junior for them. They reminded me that I was a kid and they had mastered the art here at Edi. I stared at the coffee mug in my hand given by Sinish, and I was just thinking about smashing down on the tile floor when I heard a voice behind me.

"What happened brother? You all right?" I moved on to the stairs where Guru Bhai called me, but I had decided not to talk with any of those seniors. They were all the same. He called me twice and pulled my hand while I was passing by. He saw tears in my eyes.

I turned around slowly, tears springing to my eyes. "I'm fine."

There were many thoughts revolving around in my mind but I did not have a single word to utter.

When you are injured, an ointment helps you to cure your wounds but when someone under a situation like this hurts you, no ointment is available. It's just the falling of tears that make your heart feel lighter.

I moved towards the classrc n for the fourth lecture. My batch mates were surprised to see "The unexpected Dev" in the fourth lecture. I remained silent and started paying attention to what was going on in the class.

But, I discovered my self so much poor that I couldn't even pay attention.

I thought to keep the matter aside and continue with my routine work.

It was 1am and I was sitting in the lobby with no sleep in my eyes. Puneet's words were bursting in my ears and more than that, Sinish's slap buzzing around like drum beats so loudly that sleep vanished, leaving me tensed.

Suddenly Yogi came from behind, lighting his cigarette. He passed a smoke ring in the air. May be he wanted me to look over his art but then he came in front of my eyes catching them red. As if, somebody had sprinkled chili powder. They were wet with emotions poring out. He sat besides me and asked me the reason why was I looking upset. Like an elderly brother, he picked out smoothly and softly the inside story from my heart. However, it was a great relief for me to talk, but not for Yogi.

He pulled me up, and took me to Puneet and Viral. "Who is the son of a bitch speaking against my brother?"

I told Yogi to leave the topic but he was in a bad mood.

Finally, Sinish who was silent until then, yet, spoke out.

"Yes man, I slapped him. I said those cheap words and I have no regrets. I want to kick him out of our group".

"He is just a kid and too young for all this", Viral too exclaimed looking into my eyes.

"Why all of a sudden like this"? Yogi demanded. "Did he say or do anything wrong." I started to move away. I thought about why they were doing all this and that too, with a person who was so dear to them till yesterday. The person who was running with them on an equal spirit, suddenly it seemed as if he was fractured and others want to kick him out.

I asked a question to myself. "Was I so bad that I have become a stone found inside their yummy food?"

The reason was clear.

Being a good guy was like being Saurav Ganguly. "No matters how many victories he has achieved for the country".

"No matter how many moments he has turned happy for them. People will remember the world cup he missed."

I could easily spot myself like Saurav being in the same tough situation. No matter how many moments I have turned for them happy. They just remember the one, in which I failed. But regardless of all this was there any such situation where I served my self as a bone inside their chicken. Yogi was still fighting for me. Actually, he was also eager to find out the reason behind the mess.

Finally, I shouted, "Stop it, you guys."

Though the farewell was a few weeks apart, I decided to speak my last words to the dudes.

It was time to be away, without any reason.

Hey guys,

The joy of life is being together but now your togetherness does not include me. No matters if the feelings have changed with time. There was a time when day started with you people without any end. I will remember the same for the time being.

No regrets from my side. Have a good life.

Asta lavista.

With tears in my eyes, I made a gentle move. I was waiting for a response to stop me but it seemed like my own world has grounded like an absolute halt. Silence did not break. Climbing the stairs I turned up to see what was going behind. Actually, I was still in the trauma about the seniors playing the worst joke with me. Nevertheless, they moved to their respective rooms like a calm breeze after a noisy rainfall.

That night I experienced the practical phase of life where there was no place for relations. One always has to find a gap between sentiments and being practical. Experience makes a man perfect and I was learning with such experiences day by day.

The tenderness of my heart was getting tougher after each tragic end. All the tragedies – i.e. Jasmine's matter, the seniors departed, the party, can you find the moral behind all these stories? If you could have the essence of what I did, you would have learned the amazing moral of life also.

"Every story has a tragic end, if it's not then that might just be a beginning"

The day of farewell was near and everybody at Edi was busy with some or the other stuff to make the 8th convocation for PGBDBEM-MN a successful event as they could. The staff, the students, and the faculties were engaged in making schedules about the event going to take place. Finally, it was time for the eighth batch to depart.

It was the convocation day.

The junior batch decided to throw a party for the seniors as it was their last day.

In addition, the positions and the authorities were to be handed over. Atmosphere of fun was created so that the seniors don't burst out with emotions. The spirit was high and everybody came together to cheer the last moment. But there was one person who was least interested, because he had started being selfish.

"Changes are great but changes of this kind are disastrous."

I didn't feel it wise to see them at all. Everybody was enjoying and so were the dudes but somewhere inside their heart emptiness was occupying its own space. May be because each one was going to depart after the convocation. The life, which they had spent together, was a bit careless. However, time had arrived to raise their steps to enter their respective worlds with the life style of a common man. They were going to miss each other, but the person whom everybody would be missing in common, was I.

Suddenly it was noticed at the party that I was missing. Calls after calls from most of them started to ring.

But the cell phone was buzzing inside Rajesh's pocket. I had decided to keep a distance with them, the farewell, and the party. With my laptop, I moved much earlier to my secret hide out.

A place nobody knew except me.

When I was not seen, everybody got worried. They started to search for me. Two hours passed and still seventy of them could not find the one who was disappearing from the scene. I was busy with my music and assignments.

"Silence guys" demanded Sinish. After a few minutes he uttered, "Guys did you hear something? It's Dev's favorite song - *Kesaria Balam.*"

Follow the music vibes and will get to see him. They knew what the matter was. Sinish, Puneet, Viru, and Viral moved while others were signaled to stay back.

They followed the music and reached the last corner of Edi. Restricted areas were connecting the pathway but they went on. From the corner following the vibes they reached the backyard of library.

Climbing the stairs they almost reached the top where they could see the whole of Edi at a glance. Music was getting louder and louder into their ears. There was a dome connected to a ladder on the top. The terrace was connected to a floor base. Climbing the ladder through the pathway of the floor base they reached the end.

Finally, they found me there on the roof with one leg folded and the other one waving in the air.

"Are you here to jump?" Viru shouted looking at me.

I got a horrified feel on sudden prompt of his. It was very dark so everybody switched on their mobile phones' lights. I was shocked to see them, as the place could not be easily found.

"Come on dude! Others are waiting for you at the party," Viral whispered gazing around the darkness.

"I am not in a mood, you guys carry on," I said with a low tone. "And Ya if others are keen on knowing the reason behind you guys could explain pretty well."

A chilled wave passed through them listening to my words. Sinish knew that he was guilty of whatever he has said to me. He burst out in tears. His tears were saying something. All the spirit turned into emotions. Not because they were going to leave tomorrow but they could not see me like this.

I was startled to see the tense, sorrowful expression on his face.

Finally, Sinish spoke out.

"Listen Bhai we are not against you but it's difficult to make you understand the practical phase of life."

When you are with us, you are losing your batch mates. We will leave tomorrow and your life will become like a scare crow standing all alone in the field. The SAGAR'C has screwed you up and even that fucking Mirchi Seth is back on your ass. Try to be friendly with those jerks by changing according to their attitude.

Till you are with us you won't dare to change.

Tomorrow you will find none of us. Our life at Edi has been great but it's over now. See, it has been three months and groups have started being formed. Look at the people around you. Do you find any body who will even ask a cup of coffee to you except your brother?

"The real joy of life is in togetherness man", that what you told dev.

You know what your problem is!" you want to live with each and every individual, chat, share and hang around but check if they need the same. You are loosing your value and it is difficult to recover after you have lost it.

"I have no intension to hurt but all this is for your own good health," his voice cracked. I could see he had trouble, holding back his tears.

In response I stood up and hugged Sinish awkwardly. This was upsetting. What he said made my eyes fill up. But I knew tears were coming –I lifted my chin and let the tears go at the same time.

The words were very true, I never thought about. I was just living my life and while I was doing so, things like this were completely out of my mind.

I found that the dudes were so right. I hugged all of them because from the next day, I was going to miss them all.

Puneet had his last laugh joking about the place I was sitting.

However, they used to boast about the *khopchas* in the beginning but they actually missed to find this one. After an hour, we returned to our hostel. Everybody was waiting to kick my ass as I had already spoiled the party mood.

Before any body could point me out, "I'm sorry to interrupt the party's mood," I stammered in a tiny, frightened voice. The party started with more of emotions and less of fun because after three hrs it would be 6am. Dj Parin was going back to Chennai boarding a 6:30 flight. I thought it was right time for my farewell speech which I had prepared.

I stood up to say some words. The words were in a poetic form, accumulating the journey of three months spent with the dukes.

Janglo ke beech khadi hai yeh imarat,
Jisme chhupi hui hai aap logo ke shararat,
Gaur se dekho yeh aasma chhoo rahi hai,
Talli hone ke baad sabki nazre keh rahi hai.

Zindgi thi usse jiye ja rahe the,
Tequilla ke ghunt piye ja rahe the,
Ham (9th batch) aaye phir se bahar bahar aaye,
Warna apne aap ko tassali diye ja rahe the.

Kuch aaye muskurate hue chehre, to kuch masti bare chehre,
kuch udaasi bhare chehre to kuch sharmate chehre,
Par in chehro ke piche kya tha kisi ko nahi pata
Aarma kitne gehre the kisiko nahi pata

Nayee nayee woh batein thi, Nayee nayee mulakate thi,
Badi badi batein karne ki ichha, Naye naye josh dikhane ke ichha,

Kaha woh josh thande pad gaye,
Projects aur presentations mein mannde pad gaye,
Zindgi ho gaye thi behaal istereh,
Lag reha tha jaise gand mein dande pad gaye.

Yaad hai woh chandni raat, Hath mein thi nashe ke pyali,
Woh handsome handsome londe, Woh munh mein gali,
Woh ciggerate ke dhuae mein dhal rehai thi jawani,
Yehai se suru hui hamari mehfil ki kahani.

Woh Yogi ke mastani chaal , Hawa mein laharate Punit ke baal,
Laekin Gopi ke mujhre ki... Alag hai kuch baat.

Woh Sinish ka rona, Uska imotional bloody fool hona,
Woh dosto ka manana, Phir ek peg pilana.

Woh sangeet ka tandav, Woh bin badal barsat,
Woh kichad mein lipti thi mad-mast jawani,
Zindgi thi us dhun mein deewani.

"Jisse sun rehai ho aap meri zubani
Yeh to hai hamari mehfil ki kahani"

Lakin ab,
Jis mehfil mein aap nai usse kaise sajau
Masti ke us aalam ko rangeen kaise banau
Door chale jaoge kal ham sabhi ko chhod ke
Kaise sajau un baatoko woh rang rangili raato ko

Meri mehfil adhuri si hai aapke bina....
Mehfil adhuri si hogi aapke bina....

The dudes couldn't stop their falling tears. Tears brimmed in their eyes and ran down wrinkled cheeks.

Sinish cried in a shrill startled voice. The horror of truth was sinking in. He gazed unhappily at me.

"I — I only hope that you enjoy your time in future", he said keeping his voice soft and low and hugged me.

"I don't believe this, I really don't believe," I murmured. You guys are going away far in the world which will make everybody apart.

"Not so far," Sinish said. "Just a few kilometers". Everybody laughed even in a crying emotion. "For them only three things mattered the most, love, respect and friends".

We close our eyes to pray, cry and laugh because most of the beautiful things in life are unseen and can only be felt. But I cried with open eyes because I feared that the dukes might vanish any time now.

I started to say something — but stopped. I struggled to hold back my tears. "This is so awful"! I cried

I promised myself that I would write... "I will write about us, about those crazy days we all lived at Edi. Each time they will pick my book they will miss this dear boy. A memory of life time because I believed only time fades away memories stay back"

Their legs trembled with fear because their beautiful story was going to end emotionally. All made me feel as if I were running through a dream.

"Do you know what the true story behind being an entrepreneur is"? They need to make a choice. A kind of between work and friends. They knew that if they choose work they would have to leave the community of friends making them a secondary aspect in their lives. They wished if the journey would have been extended a year more but god does not fulfill all our wishes.

Sinish made everybody cry.

If you want to realize the value of one second, ask either one who has escaped from an accident or the guys who were starving for it. They wished to hold the time but it was passing so fast that everyone felt helpless. They have no others option except catch their beautiful memories in mind with the photographs and videos in DVD's.

I was surprised to see the situation. It has been a year since these people were together. Such a bonding was amazing. I always wished to live such phase of a life with my batch mates. This incident became a dream after the seniors went away because the joy of shedding tears for a person whom you are going to miss all your life is much more fascinating than anything in life. There is always a hope that one day we will meet again. With a new life back with those memories sipping a cup of coffee together chatting about the golden days, how we had lived with the spirit to the fullest.

ACT 5

Power attracts the corruptible

The most beautiful thing in this world is to see your friend smiling and you know the next best thing is to discover that you are the reason behind that smile. I never knew when the dudes became the reason for my smile. They went away leaving a mark of sadness amongst us. Those boys had carved their joy in the bricks of Edi where even the rains couldn't erase it.

That Evening...

"*Ohh... fuck,*" Abhinav shouted when a water splash came from the first floor. It was Aniket, the animal from Ranchi. Abhinav ran towards him. I think that ignited him. However, he didn't know that Modi was standing behind the walls with another bucket of water. That splash by Modi wiped away all our tears of separation.

It was bath time with a different mood.

Soon nudity prevailed amongst the boys at Edi lawn. Everybody was so lost into the mood that they became least bothered about the Uzbek gals watching the scene. A batch from Uzbekistan has just arrived for a one-month entrepreneurship program. It was no surprise when they started to capture the dirtiest of all in their cameras. While brats like Vivek and Modi gave modeling pose for their macho look, Abhinav and I thought it wise to hide our balls.

Happiness seemed shorter when our eyes caught a figure running towards us. He was a man of medium height, with a puffy face and little eyes. Of course after that illegal act the security guard was not going to leave us so easily. He rushed to Aniket who was busy sprinkling water on his crotch.

"Give me that pipe you rascal. Is it's your grand pa's resort"? The guard shouted on top of his voice. Aniket collected his shampoo and body wash to complete the evening bath inside the three walled bathroom. But for Abhinav it was again time to do something of his kind. He went to the first floor bathroom and got a few buckets of water to continue the leisure. Sooner the hostel lawn became a bare land with muddy water all over and no grass at all.

Aniket who was standing downstairs got hype in excited that he covered his whole body with mud. His naughtiness didn't leave us neat. Suddenly something started to itch inside Aniket eyes. Poor guy cried for water unaware about the war which was going to take place in the environment.

"The war was between the good and the bad odor of smell."

It was very clear that the exotic smell came from the fragrance of mud but what about the bad odor. No body knew about the scene when Abhinav did a public display. Aniket who was standing downstairs starving for water experienced the worst joke of his life. The scene was so disgustingly performed by Abhinav that left the bad odor win the battle.

"You know he actually pied on the poor boy."

A few minutes later Aniket discovered the bullshit thing that had happened to him. He now felt like being raped many times and then left untouched. The next day it was masala news to be discussed among all. Even the girls got an email personally from Mirchi Seth about the incident. Innocent Aniket didn't have a word to utter because now that fun was created at his cost.

Hi friends...

Here is the third Edition of Garam Masala... Hope u enjoy it...

MIRCHI MAILS

TUjHE mIRChI LAgEE TO MeiN KyA KarUN

(If you caught the chili, what should I do?)

Hi Dudes and the so called babes of the 9th batch. This is the third edition of Garam Masala.

Mirchi Seth is back with Mirchi updates.... I know u guys have been waiting since long for this.......... But friends! Patience pays.

To start with, our Netaji ... the bluff master Abhinav ... is really a disgusting person who played with a poor boy's feelings.

Aniket the animal from Ranchi is now searching a new identity after the older being pied by Abhinav.

Ankul... has come back from Tirupati temple with a brand new Sabu look (bald) ... a guy who actually is a hosteller yet seems to be at home only with books???...

Chirayu, a studious chap ... a man of few words ... his life revolves around Castor oil ... the oil used as lubricant in his ass... we don't know what he is up to.

Ashish... the magician (the invisible dog) ... a wanna be.... Who in order to impress his new chick was doing stunts on his bike ... but ended up throwing her on the road helpless.

Payal ... the lady in black ... really leaves a wowooo on many of our south Indians fans when she enters the hall with her purse dangling ... but it seems she does not care for their feeling.... She walked out of there group assignments as if they were untouchables ... I can understand they got dark complexion but 'blacks' it's a disgusting title.

Sameer Patel... has lost his voice, he rarely speaks ... is this because the boys have given him a kick from behind, or is he missing Kanta Bhabi.

Kalpesh has trapped a jumbo African double his age ... and is always busy with her ... A couple of Durex condoms were found outside his room... He seems to have tasted the blood in his room. It's advisable to throw the same in backyard and keep the campus neat.

Modi the famous ... who has lost all his wealth in *Satta(betting)* ... was caught in a new scandal with Rajesh Jhawar .... They were caught cheating and Mr. Shah who received Xerox copied answers from the two, ended up giving doses for an hour.

Vishal... The consultant guy.... Let me tell u he can help you out with any type of problems and convince you on the same ...specially girls'.... He is the girl's consultant.

Vivek... a big time flirt, does not leave any girl, untouched ... weather it's a kamwali bai of girl's hostel.

Shiven ... carries a great sense of humor always hits a six without a bat...

Vanshi ... the darling of back bencher's... has a whole lot of fans to her list... Her birthday was filled with chocs ... cakes ... flowers ... leaving many girls jealous ... burnt to asses...

Anna... he really gets into the characters of the novels he reads and can be seen shouting in his dreams ... the dialogs like "*Bachoo Bachooo – SAVE ME SAVE ME.*" He makes all sorts of noises scaring everybody except Sid.

It's a fact discovered about Sid who lies in bed shaking so hard when the lights are off that he knocked a lamp off his nightstand.

Priyanka.... She has a whole bunch of lovers on her list ... she has a fan in every room of the boys hostel ... we don't know for sure, but Abhinav literally screwed that sweet girl for a sandwich... how could Abhinav do this.

Mr. Rakshit ... a rare piece.... Who has his own set of theories..... Lives in his own world ... love in his own ways... Celebrated his B'day in a rare way spending the whole night inside jungle all alone.... He is a real case study.

Like a dog's, tail can not be straightened... in the same way Gaurang's sickness cannot be cured ... a real good guy but cannot see anything else when the girls are around.

Jasmine.... is hunting for a new one.... Something is cooking.... It can be smelled.

Hahahahhhhhhhhhaaaaaaaaaaaaaaaa.... Enjoy every minute, the real taste of Edi till the next Mirchi mail hits your inbox ... GOOD LUCK, we really need it.

Mirchi mails are just created for fun. It does not intend to harm anyone. Mirchi Seth has high regards for everyone. No hard feelings.

U can always write back to me ... For any suggestion ... Best effort will be made to include your suggestion.

Aniket did not turn up to the classroom for a week. Embarrassment turned the animal guy into a puppet. All his energy level failed to regain after that incident. Finally, it was a question mark amongst all as whatever Abhinav did was ethical or unethical. Moreover, it was blamed upon Mirchi Seth to exaggerate the situation.

Who was Mirchi Seth? Why was he doing all this? Is he Ankul or Modi or mischievous Abhinav? Everybody used to live together, then where these-mails came from? These were a few question marks no body knew the answer. While all this was going, can you find a true fact that prevailed at Edi?

"Fun was created at the cost of an individual not at the cost of a moment".

It was already a week since the seniors departed. We were directed to shift our luggages to the new hostel rooms where seniors used to live earlier. Selection of rooms and room partners were totally choice based. The rooms were only ten while the students were forty.

That was an easy division but, *"For the first time Vivek, Vishal, I, Rajesh and Ritesh had a tough mathematical division to face."* We all wanted to live together but only four could adjust. The situation demanded sacrifice but whom? We all went to Sillu to get rid of the tension, and have a cup of tea. Silence prevailed among all the boys.

Vanshi banged all of a sudden with chocolates and a cute smile on her face. Our faces seemed more like one in funeral.

Hey guy's wass... up! You all look tensed. Anything I can help.

When brats like Vivek could not get the solution it was least expected from Vanshi to shower a solution. There is nothing worse than silence, strung like heavy beads on too delicate conversations like this. In that small period of time when I had borne the pain of separation from Sinish and Puneet this little one made no difference.

I thought hard before I answered. "Guys! I think it's me. It makes no difference to depart rooms when our hearts are still one and united"

Rajesh took my side and decided to join me leaving Vivek, Vishal, and Ritesh in room no. 35. The five of us always wished to create our dominance as equivalent as SAGAR'C. After the separation, life changed a lot. Vivek and Vishal seemed more furious in the race, and went far with their destinations. From now onwards they were linked up with Modi and group and acted as active committee members.

Second semester exams were soon to began. Exam fever occupied our brains. We were missing the illegal advices from seniors. Days passed like *Satabdi Express* with financial management open book exam on top of the chart. The concept didn't seem as simple as it looks like. *"Even if we would have dug the whole of Edi then also we were not going to find the hidden answers."* Prof. Upadhaya couldn't be underestimated. While the rest started to note every word with a magnifying glass the SAGAR'C came out with an idea, which nobody could even, dare to think.

The night was silent. I was on the other side of terrace with a lamp, a vodka bottle and a few account books to battle with the senses.

While lying there I wondered if I weren't here studying financial management and would have been an astronomer. It would demand too much math here also for my brains, I know that, but there was always been something good about charting the stars that appealed to me rather than heavy lumpy books. On a really dark night, I could see thousand stars or may be million more that haven't been discovered. It would be so easy to think that the world revolves around you, but all you have to do is staring up at the sky to realize it isn't that way at all.

My thoughts broke when I heard voices, 'whispering voices' from the SAGAR'S room. Their talks seemed to be floating through their room.

The voices grew louder as I made my way to the room. They were actually planning to go to the Xerox room at Edi. It's a place where every paper, official or unofficial, is been Xeroxed at Edi. Their thinking was worth millions.

"May be the exam papers were Xeroxed and kept there lying to be dispatched tomorrow", Modi said.

It was just a hope.

Modi, Gaurang, Vishal and Vivek went to check it out, without giving a hint to the other members of SAGAR'C. The Xerox room was locked. I followed them all, giving no clue of my presence. They tried to break the lock but in vain.

Finally, Modi took a stone and broke the glass of a window. He managed to open the window's knob and got into the room. One by one all got inside with no noise at all. They searched the whole store, but found nothing. After half an hour of checking into the documents lying there, they planned to leave.

"It's truly said that wrong ideas blink inside your head faster than the good ones".

It was Vivek again with his triple O certificate. After all he was a computer engineer how he could leave the main clue.

He whispered silently, "Guys this is a p3400 series Japanese machine with multiple scanning, auto saving save and printing options."

"If we knew this much in life there wouldn't have been a situation to steal an exam paper" Modi said as everybody else bursted out into laughter.

This machine always scans a document first before printing. This means before printing, every document moves to the main memory replacing the older one. While we were searching for the papers, have you realized that there might be a soft copy left inside? If we are lucky enough, the last document, Xeroxed should be our paper for tomorrow's financial management's exam. "So what do you say? Shall I start the machine for the final check up?" he said glancing around.

No one needed another thought to shake their head in assent.

Within minutes, he succeeded in his idea. His instinct was right. Vivek glances up over the rim of the paper. It was lying as a soft copy, which just needed a print command. I heard Vishal shouting with joy after getting the paper.

But Vivek didn't seem to hear. His eyes were locked on the entrance. Modi followed the glance.

"Ohh." a horrified moan escaped his throat as he saw a tall-fat ass guard with snapping brown eyes magnified by thick glasses marching towards him.

A heavy feeling of dread started in Vishal's stomach. His mouth dropped open and his chin started to quiver.

"What is going on here"? The guard shouted with a roaring voice. He studied them for a moment but before he could speak, Modi quickly deposited a few thousands in his pocket.

"Welcome to India my friend" It's the best possible way to get away! Modi and Vivek succeeded in their own ways to get the final solution to their problems. I was peeping from behind the wall looking over the deeds of the losers. But then I thought not to interfere, keeping it a secret inside my heart.

It was 3 am in clock and the sleep creeping on in my eyes. Suddenly a loud noise lashed into my ears, breaking the sleepy mood. I came out of my room and saw Abhinav shouting. I went to their room and closed the doors. What was the matter was still a mystery to me.

"You are not invited here so better leave the room", Gaurang passed his statement.

"Is the paper leak scandal much more important for you than my presence?" They were shocked to hear the words. But it wasn't time to explain how I got to know all the fuss. What was important was the dispute between Gaurang and Abhinav. Men become selfish after achieving the materialistic pleasures of life. A greedy man cannot even see good things happening to others. Gaurang was one of those greedy people who wanted to have the paper all alone and secure good marks win the best student's award and get the prize of 60k. His thoughts were cheap hiding the only paper from his very dear friends in order to skip publicizing. When Modi protested that under whatsoever situation, he will share the paper with Abhinav; there was Abhinav who has the same condition for Ankul and Shiven. The list continued with Rajesh and me having a strong link up with Ankul.

Abhinav lost his temper on Gaurang's selfishness. Lately, Gaurang cried for this mistake but it was now difficult to make Abhinav understand.

He passed a statement, "Your selfish interests have crossed all limits. Now, you do one thing. Pass on the paper to every student or I will puke the shit out of your ass in front of the director"

Abhinav left in silence leaving a tensed situation for the other members. If they uttered a single word about the scandal, not only their image was going to be shattered, but also there was a possibility of being expelled out of Edi. A thought clicked inside my mind. Rajesh's was quite good in financial management and I wanted him to solve the situation.

The idea was simple. As it was an open book exam, we will distribute pamphlets to everybody in the name of course material.

The next day the same leaked paper was given to us. Everybody was amazed to see the actual answers in the pamphlets but no dumbs could find the hidden meaning. It took hardly 30 min to complete a 3 hours question paper. Prof Upadhaya was shocked to find no query being raised by a single student.

The matter was then buried providing no hint about what has actually happened.

Abhinav was a man of principles. He now felt suffocated inside the group he had created. With him, Ankul and Shiven too left the group. After exams it was time to step in the shoes of our seniors.

Committees were formed and responsibilities were distributed amongst selected students. Gaurang got the power to rule mess committee. He was responsible to fix the menu for lunch, dinner, and break fast but then it simply became a one man show. Many a time it was seen that the choice of ingredients inside the menu were solely amongst his favorites. SAGAR'C experienced VIP treatment in Gaurang's company.

The mess management was getting political.

In a leading entrepreneurship institute like Edi where everybody came to learn the art of business, Gaurang had already learned that earlier.

The logic was quite simple.

On Sundays, watching a movie and munching dinner outside was preferred among students. If Edi provided 93 rupees per student for eatables a day how much Mukeshji could have saved on a Sunday?

Gaurang used to give Mukeshji the information about those students who were going to have food outside. The basic scene behind cost cutting was to prepare less food in view of absentees and to give half the benefit from its savings to the committee members in terms of VIP servings.

On the other hand, may be his selfishness took all the decisions. Whatever it was, but I could say these three things for him —

1. His post defined his caliber and his selfishness defined his intensions
2. His mind defined his knowledge but the use defined his untrustworthiness
3. Every man has a right to think about his leisure and so he did but at the cost of other's (wishes)?

Everybody knew his intensions but nobody pointed his finger at him to prove him wrong. Nevertheless, one day there was a person standing all alone to show mess politics in its true picture.

It's truly said, "An iron can cut another iron."

23rd October, 1:53pm.

It was nearly noon and I was still in the pajamas: never thought to take a change of my clothes. I went for lunch in the mess. While I was moving, my nose caught a delicious odor of baked Swiss cake. A cake in this jungle was something unexpected. I ran to grab one of my share before my moth got flood up with water.

"Swiss cake first" I demanded to the chef giving a beggar's look as if didn't had good food for months. The staff boy went inside to take it. It was ten minutes when nobody turned up I thought to give a check.

"Mukeshji its heights of carelessness. I'm waiting since last ten minutes like a leopard for his hunt"

"Its over Dev, you are gain late" Mukeshji got his eyes out of me yawning.

"But its still time" I urged

"It wasn't in the menu but a special serving from our side". With a sad mood, I left picking up the same cold chapattis with yellow lump in my plate. A few minutes later Abhinav came demanding the same. I think we both had a dog's nose.

"No option buddy! Some hungry mother fucker has gulped our Swiss cake. "*Bhagwan! Bhen de tako ka paet kharab ho jaye*"

"We have no other option in this forest" Abhinav said giving up his eager mood and sat with me scooting a chair closer to me to have lunch.

Abhinav was a kind of person who wants every thing ready made. Whether its class assignment or food. He would always be dreaming about the person who will feed him with the golden spoon. After lunch, we went to our rooms. When we were moving, we met

Gaurang and group on the way. SAGAR'C was no more in existence. I said to Abhinav about the mess politics. Later on, I added a one-liner, which banged like havoc in Abhinav's mind.

I simply prompted, "If the cake was over where the smell came from."

The point was worth thinking. Though the odor was invisible but its source couldn't be.

Abhinav stopped for a while, his eyes wide open. We both turned back to the mess. When we entered, we saw the same Swiss cake in Gaurang's plate. Abhinav's head turned his acts wild like a ghost. His head busted in anger. After all he was a former ABVP president how could he leave the situation so easy? The opposition has cheated him and now it was a matter of self-respect and prestige.

He dashed on Mukeshji holding his collar. His voice no longer remained like a feather. *"Machudawni... juth kya bolyo."*

His voice was tough with that Marwadi accent and was easily visible from the fear reflected in Mukeshji's eyes. He knew he was in fault and there was no excuse for it.

Modi ran to hold Abhinav and control his anger but all in vain.

It occupied an hour with eight hands to make the furious Abhinav settle his anger. But the matter didn't find a settling way. Even Modi's explanations could not satisfy his ego. It only showed how much he was hurt.

Finally, when everybody connected tried to suppress the issue Abhinav started a Satyagrah movement.

"A of movement in favor of all the students who were a victim of mess politics".

He announced that he will not have food in mess until Mukeshji is there in management. It was a tough decision but not as tough as you are thinking. Actually it wasn't ***hunger strike*** one which you got to watch in movies but he started eating outside at times of lunch and dinner. The scene became regular. Every time Abhinav was late, he had an excuse that he was out for lunch.

Management at Edi was in a double minded situation of throwing Mukeshji out but that will bring legal issues. They have signed a contract with the caterers and so it could not be breached.

On the other hand, the PG chair people personally apologized for the deed and asked Abhinav to leave the Satyagrah. He was very accurate with his words and for no reason he would leave the movement which he started.

One-day Abhinav asked me to have dinner outside with him.

I joined him on his wish. We went to *Shiv Shakti* a near by *dhaba* to have our favorite *Khichdi.* The dinner was light but wonderful. On the way, I pulled the brakes of my bike near the Narmada dam's bridge. The bench on the side of the bridge was our favorite destination to chill out. I wanted to talk and convince him to leave the Satyagrah. I asked him what the problem was after the chairperson personally apologized to him. I knew him well. He would not accept the chairperson's apology. He wanted to end the mess politics at any cost because he believed in doing instead of thinking.

"Dev do you know what is the difference between you and me?" He questioned me. I thought why he was asking me such brain storming questions. I remained silent. So silent as if I just wanted only him to speak. He was carrying a pound load inside his heart. May be he wanted to say something to me as if he really cared about me after all. He then speaking solemnly.

Abhinav spoke...

Do you believe in the concept of branding? I don't know about you but I actually do. Branding is an important chapter of marketing and so is the one for our lives. If you want to be known among the society, you have to do something to get into focus. I created my own brand at Edi in the name of 'Dagaji'. One has to market himself, may be for the reason of prestige or for being a center of attraction, as you did on the very first day. People seemed to talk only about you as if you are some sort of genie who is going to fulfill their wishes.

I have certain ethics and people respect me for that. Now this incident was a controversy against my ethics and I strongly opposed that. If I step back today, next time this brand "Abhinav" will not work. The next time people will not take me seriously, if I raise any kind of issue because today I failed to serve my purpose.

The same thing happened to you also but did you care about it. When you came at Edi, I wanted to be you. I wished to live your life. But after everything got worse I feel pity you. You should rule others; let not people rule your life. Can you even make others convince of your thought?"

"The problem is not around you but it's inside you."

Inside your own empty mind. You can't run away from it. You can't hide from it. And now you cannot even solve it. His words were making my legs shiver.

That day I got the meaning of her words. *"Dev, you never tried to understand things."*

People shattered my brand image and I did not even bother to correct.

With me, I was also giving a wrong impression of her in the eyes of others. She didn't want to loose me because I was the only friend she got. Today I solved the riddle which Jasmine had placed but now it was too late. Because of me, today we were not even in talking terms. It felt like a stab thinking about the only friend I lost. That night I had my deepest thoughts for her in a poetic form.

The Mountain Girl - Revisited (The death bed)

Yet again like the falling sky the lightening cracked and gave a cry
My soul awoke from an incomplete sleep and it happened when I felt like die

Death for the mortal being but love that would have always been,
Carrying my life she gave a sight that mountain girl
with all her might

Years like had passed since I met her first and years will pass with this lovely thirst
To conquer her heart and kiss her soul with a undying desire to achieve that goal

Nature put at shame before her when she casts her radiant smile
Even the flowers feel charm less before her stunning style

Nothing has changed in these months this has any significance with our lovely knot

She waited for me to come back to her till then she enjoyed
what she never got

Tears rolled down her lovely cheeks though it was very hard to see
Rain splashed her shining smile which now went far away miles?

The surroundings gave a cheerful call the moment was great but
small
She always loved me her eyes did tell but without her now life is hell

But as it was against nature's law our name be always taken together
she stepped towards me to hug my soul but alas the scene changed
its goal

My heart was joyous just a few seconds back but a sudden pain
engulfed its walls
I knew I was about to die in pearl Leaving behind that lovely girl

But the race was already lost though it was more than an obvious win
We could be together all these days though the chances were quiet thin

I realized my dreams though it was tough Happiness will enrobe me
even on my death bed
And only when I meet her my last tear will shed.

No matter what she is now and how our relationship is, before all that, she was my best friend. A tiny cry escaped from me. I thanked Abhinav for whatever he said. He gave me a true lesson that I will never forget. Today's community can be divided into three categories - The good, the bad, and the ugly.

So when there were people like Abhinav who had a different perception about how to develop himself as a brand, there were also people like Gaurang who branded themselves in a mixed manner where it was difficult to define his particular image. Abhinav played true politics with social interest and personal well-being while Gaurang played real politics with selfish interest to get to the position he was in. I was among those ugly people who were immature and impractical.

ACT 6

The other side of an unexpected hero

It was already two months for Abhinav but he wasn't in any mood to quit the purpose for which he was doing Satyagrah.

He thought the needful to get the creeps out. On the other hand power made Gaurang perform corrupt practices in order to retain the position. The mango people at Edi did not feel it was important to support nor did they felt to fight. They just wanted peace, away from the power and politics played. May be they were right or may be coward but at the end there was only one sufferer –"Abhinav". I wondered on whose leg Abhinav was smashing that axe. It was a mystery which I thought would only end after he got out of the havoc. Till then our lives continued with another picture of life phases.

The emergence of fun buried the frolic stage created by Abhinav.

The next day it was our industrial visit to Havmor industry. We were supposed to meet Minakshi Mam at 7am sharp on the reception counter. The same day, Gaurang threw a party.

No matter who is involved but when it comes to partying people never stepped back. The sky was falling and the earth seemed drenched. With every peg of vodka the mood got wilder. The security guard at the hostel area was the only one in senses. He came rushing to us as a dog.

"Bhen de tako... aaj kher nahi tumri", He came with a rod more kind of an ancient wooden stick our grand parents use to keep for support. I caught his red eyes. Though the color was black but they became red with anger. I had a close eye on his mustache which seemed it has grew into one *dara singh* had. Money is the god for all evils. It took hardly four pegs and a few hundreds too silent the guard.

Everybody present decided to continue the *bhakchodi* until its time for our industrial visit but then they didn't know the tiny drops of liquid they just had were going to explode like atom bombs inside. The plan was good. Till four the mood continued with twenty people. Others either slept or the vodka made them pass out on the ground. We continued the party with our beer bottles. Mad heads Modi, Gaurang, Ritesh, Sid and me had some strange ideas till we fell asleep and sun arrived with a happy morning. What happened next was a mystery for us but what seemed strange was the environment around with more of bra's hanging and less of mess around. It was strange to our minds when we actually realized to have ended up inside girl's hostel.

Get up you ass hole, you almost buried me under your legs, Anastha screamed while dragging as she found herself struggling for breadth.

"Oh..!" my mouth left open looking at her. She was wearing a sleeveless nightwear seemed it was one of a fat ass lady with light pink shorts showing her waxed legs. "You could win first prize in Baywatch contest" I said looking at her with my mouth open and eyes broader than the mouth.

"You are such a jerk", she shouted.

"How the hell I got here"? I demanded an answer.

"Ask your jerk buddies", she said pointing me to Gaurang and Modi who were lying on each other. I photographed that *dostana* pose for more face book comments.

"Oh my god" I puked the water on the fat ass Sid's face suddenly when I realized she was wearing my waist.

"Bull shit… it's eight" Modi reminded us of the industrial visit. We ran towards our hostel area with me in semi naked attire hiding from the eyes of the professor who was waiting for us at the reception counter. She was puzzled to see only two girls ready for the visit. It became a matter of shame for her. She herself moved with the idea of getting the nuts out.

When she entered the boy's hostel area, she was shocked to see Shiven and Ajay sleeping in the lawn with beer bottles all around them.

"What the hell is all this?" One more moment and the professor stormed away again, her clogs striking the tile floor like a lion's roar.

"*Chal re budhbhak! Sone de,*" Ajay replied in *Bihari* while he was still asleep. He did not see the professor at all.

She took a stick and went slowly towards Ajay and Shiven. They both were fast asleep. May be dreaming about hot chicks.

"AAA. Aaaa" loud noise from Ajay when he got a *zappak* on his

ass from the professor. Shiven woke up hearing that and ran towards the hostel.

The other students who were planning to skip the visit made themselves invisible. After twenty minutes when nobody came downstairs, she decided for a room check.

Room no.35 empty, 36, 37... Empty, 38, 39, 40, 41.... Empty, 42... Empty.

"Come out students", she screamed moving fast towards the bathing area.

Khadi, who was moving in his underwear inside the bathroom area, had a very bad experience. "What's going on? You bloody shameless creature" Her voice so tight it might snap. The professor clashed with him catching an eye of his almost nude position. Some students jumped towards the forest from the bathroom windows, others like us too scared to jump decided to lock ourselves inside the toilet. It was the only place left for a hide out.

"That stinks!" Sid made a nasty expression pinching his nose expecting mogra smell to come from inside the commode.

"Dude! You only do here everyday." Ritesh replied making a fun of him.

"Oh shut up you two! I want to check whether the professor has gone or not?" I raised my head but could not see what was going on. So, I decided to stand on the commode and look for her. It was difficult for all five of us to fit in a single toilet.

"Is the professor still there or has she left?" Abhinav asked me.

I indicated him to be silent. A few seconds later, I raised my head standing on the commode to look around. My concentration was all on her on what was she doing.

Suddenly Sid made a move and my leg slipped inside the commode.

"Fuck!" I shouted, making an angry look. A little voice can break the silence but from my side it was a roar.

The professor discovered human presence inside. While all the other four bathrooms were open, she knocked the fifth one and commanded us open.

Finally, we had to listen to her because she won the hide & seek game. We opened the door with eyes down; legs squeezed and raised hand for an apology.

"Breaking news -future budding entrepreneurs of Edi found hiding in a bathroom for what reason? - An industrial trip" that sucks.

I felt a heavy lump inside my throat.

We apologized again and again like beggars for our behavior and got ready for the visit. She got angry on us and gave us 5 minutes to get ready.

When everybody took just four minutes, I was the one who was late again, taking 13 whole minutes and a few seconds more to get ready. Actually, it took five to wash "whose shit I don't know it was".

We rushed at the reception to conform our presence. "Move fast you late latif's", Prof. Pandey said pointing towards a non-A/C two by three *khatara* standing on the parking lobby.

"If it wasn't for marks I swear I would have jumped from the window" I murmured inside Vivek's already red ears as if they were burning.

"Then it would have been a hospital visit rather industrial one" he laughed.

"Silence you too; the professor shouted showing her eagle eyes." We cursed ourselves but later on found that the absentees would end up with negative marks in their assignments by the professor. Time passes when it wishes to pass but I think today it was against us.

"This visit sucks like masturbating in a public even though everyone is watching you do that," I said.

"Ha ha ha...Nobody here got the meaning dude. It's just for your own leisure," Rajesh replied passing the chip's packet.

"Fuck with the leisure. That's what we always did at Edi, paying lacs to an educational resort".

"So what kind of visit you want?" The professor fingered in between. Actually, she was listening to our conversation when we were chatting.

"Madam, I didn't mean that but do you find any positive outcome which will benefit us on visiting an Ice-cream factory." Abhinav's question was not only genuine but it was a sort of learning for the professor too.

"So you wanna go to China for an industrial visit?" She asked

"Bingo! You hit a million dollar jackpot", Abhinav exclaimed in surprise.

"I think he is still in a hangover", I laughed making fun.

"I have seen institutes taking students abroad for industrial visits. When we are in our home country, we can learn any time. But, an industrial visit abroad will make a big difference. Then look at the attendance and I am sure a deaf head would like to miss this opportunity." Abhinav said with a sparkling confidence in his eyes. "Impossible." I said.

"Why is it not possible?" Prof. Pandey grooved! "However, the problem is expenses are to be borne by the students. The institute can only provide you support for the idea."

"That's awesome! Modi jumped with joy". For lads of rich dad's it was another chance to go for a holiday but now I saw a change. A big changing environment where in people wanted to learn. Do something for which they were here for. Reports and presentations started being made by students on how to make an industrial visit to China successful. Shiven and Abhinav who were a part of the talk worked nights for the visit to happen. An event needs a leader to turn it successful. There were two here to promote their aspiration with the proposals along the finances. The opportunity was great, but only a son of a millionaire would be convinced.

I also planned to go for this trip. The trip was going to cost forty-five thousand and a few hundreds more. I was still in a state of confusion calculating the worth of spending thousands. The third semester was not only tough but also challenging as detailed project report was to be submitted individually. A few decided to go to China for learning so that they could make a viable project to convince the bank officials for loan. It was late when I realized that I have spent more than half a year into something unproductive. The DPR stage got more crucial. Everyone was allotted a mentor for his or her respective projects. As I always wanted to go into textiles, Prof. D. M. Waghela was on my side.

Here I came to realize the importance of a mentor, who changed my life. A real teacher is one, who takes his follower on a path, which is actually designed, for him. China trip was my wish and I wanted to go, but destiny had planned something else for me. It was at that time when I started taking life seriously. The mentor asked me a simple question, "What did you learn till now being a resident at Edi?" I could not figure out why I came to Edi. But I found that when I was all into relationships and social bonding, I actually forgot the purpose. That purpose for which I was here remained unsolved.

I therefore promised him to do whatever he asked because then I found myself quite matured enough to think about my career. When Abhinav came to know that I was not going to China, he tried every tactic to convince me. But I was moving on the right path now, which Waghela sir showed me.

The next day I went to his cabin to discuss about the project report.

I entered Prof. Waghela's office. It was Silent. I was alone in his office long enough to note that his desk was so clean; you could play mini cricket game on the desk. I took his file to have a look. I didn't notice at what moment he appeared. When the doors busted, I practically fell out of my chair. I saw him. He had black hair and was at least as tall as my dad- six feet with a right angle jaw and eyes that look frozen over.

"So you are here. Are you not going to China with rest of your batch mates?"

"No sir, I wanted to stay here and use my internship period wisely." I answered while he was still peeping into his thick glasses all over the desk.

"So tell me your field of interest?" He muttered without giving a sigh

"Sir, may I look for what you are looking". I passed an impressive thought in his mind. I thought he was looking for the amount of dandruff fallen from his scalp.

"Is it your field of interest? I thought it was something else", he joked I think balancing the mini creature on a paper. It was a tiny piece of *Gur* with ants dashing into like a party animal all over it. Throwing that outside the room he again got back to me.

"Textiles... sir! I cleared his thoughts reminding about my original interest. As my family business was related I planned my carrier with a series of expansions.

"Please elaborate" the Prof urged.

We are into... *oops* sorry! My dad is into manufacturing of cotton printed fabric used for single bed sheets, Nighty, and Salwar Suit dress materials."

"So you want to continue with him and expand your business?" he asked.

"Yes sir, I want to join him, but my plans are different."

"What plans?" he asked making a point on what I said.

"Sir, I want to move into garments. I have heard that there is a high scope and a lot of money in this field."

"Yes of course. That is true. But why are you joining your father then?"

"Sir it is a step-by-step process".

I have read that entrepreneurs are born but that's all bookish. There are entrepreneurs like me who need to be created with proper training and knowledge.

"Are you relying upon somebody"? Waghela sir marked a question on my statement.

"Who can be a better teacher than your own father"? I placed my thoughts before him.

Your father will train you in the business but who will serve his purpose in future when you actually wish to go in garment line? Why don't you visit our cluster development program at Bangalore? In addition, there is a Textile-Expo to be held which will improve your knowledge base.

"Sir, I appreciate your words and the program but is it worth? Actually I was thinking of something else. I have heard about that Denim manufacturing unit 'Arvind Mill'. It's in Bangalore. Can you help me to get into the plant to collect details about the process as well as other information?"

"Okay, let me talk to Dr. Siddesh Ansari. He will definitely help you.

"It would be great sir and I could even attend the cluster development program but I don't know anybody in Bangalore?" I muttered.

"Haven't you heard about Edi branch at Bangalore? They will guide you and fulfill all your requirements," said murderer Waghela who just smashed an ant with his news paper.

With the required information, I decided to move to Bangalore. It was a new city for me but I had made up my mind. Waghela sir truly guided me what I had to do. I emailed my requirements to Branch Edi, Bangalore.

The reply came on the day itself specifying me about the details of what I had asked.

Dear Devendra,

It is an honor for us that for the first time somebody from EDI, Ahmedabad is coming here as a student for the purpose of internship. We have made your living arrangements at 114, Somayya apartment near chinnama koil, forth crossing, fifth lane, Banna giri, Bangalore-28. The train will reach at 6am and you can come directly to the specified address paying 40 rupees to the autowala.

Regarding any assistance, you can call any time on EDI branch office. The person who would be sharing place with you is Mr. Anurag Basu and his contact is 09886076586. Have a safe journey.

Regards,

Edi, Bangalore.

Some emails annoy you but of this kind would bug your head thinking about the only lane you have to search, in order to reach the hideout. Plump kannad women's carrying no relation with sweetness may assist you wrongly and you end up on the fifth crossing forth lane instead of the reverse. I wondered what if I missed my crossing and got to another lane searching for the only house which isn't situated there. The thought gave me a 440 volt shock while the phone kept ringing waking me up from that horrible dream. But, I had decided to leave the material pleasures behind and go for the project.

I booked my tickets and moved on February 10. I penned down the phone number of Anurag at six different places who was going to share place with me. The train was on right time and I reached Bangalore sharp at six. I called Anurag to inform him that I had already reached.

"Hey, is this Anurag?" I asked his name for a conformation. I knew that that it was he but then also, I couldn't hold on my nervousness.

"Yes, speaking." he replied in an awkward tone as if scolding me for waking him up so early. It felf as if he got *Bipasa Basu* in his dream which suddenly disappeared with my buzz.

"Hi, this is Devendra from Edi, Ahmedabad. I am supposed to share the place with you."

"Oh, yes! So you are here. But dude I am in Ooty and will turn up next week."

"Where will I go man? I screamed like a helpless women. Are you crazy! I don't know anybody over here. What shall I do?" again I repeated the task of screaming in shock.

"Can't you adjust for a week? He said.

"Okay." I ended the call with a small word puked outside instead a lot more inside.

For a moment, I thought I should pay lump sum amount to the engine driver and direct him to get back to the same train and take me to Ahmedabad. But I took a cup of tea and sat on the near by bench for some refreshment. The refreshment was long. It seemed like hours have passed away.

I decided to step out of the station and move towards the auto stand. The city was over crowded with less of passengers and more of coolies and autowala's. It was a pleasant atmosphere. Not so hot, may be the sun hasn't arrived to his duty. An old boned, white beard which seemed least like a human stood in front of my eyes. "Shall I take your luggage?" I saw him head to toe. He was wearing a cotton shirt with more holes than buttons and an ultra cool natural air conditioned *lungi*.

"Leave *anna*, if you will carry my luggage who will carry you" I laughed on my own stupid joke. I carried my luggage to the prepaid auto stand.

"Where...?" a harsh voice pinched my ears.

"Some trust worthy & good hotel". While he was moving I tried to be over smart questioning him to drag nothing out.

"Where are you taking me Uncle? Take me to near by best hotel".

The place he stopped was not only pathetic but had a disgusting surrounding. The area belonged to fishermen who sold crabs, fishes and sea food items. The hotel named "Best lodge". I thought, he was taking advantage of me being a new comer to the city and took me round and round or may be English isn't easy for him to understand so I tried in Hindi to explain my needs.

"Bhaiya! Acha hotel hona...Jo bharose ke layak ho" Finally, he dropped me outside a hotel. I read the name – **Hotel Bharosa** and discovered that this guy who was driving neither knew neither Hindi nor English. He just made a guess and a fuss out of me. I paid 100 for auto rent and 1000 bucks as hotel advance. The hotel guy told, "It was just 10 rupees from the station, you have been cheated." There is no scarcity of cheaters in this world. They just need a chance to rob. But this guy was a genuine cheater. I didn't screw my mind and kept my luggage inside the hotel room.

The room was good but not as good as the hotel's name suggested. I had my bath with eyes closed and mind shut not thinking about the unhygienic water falling over me. I dressed like a party animal planning to check the nerve of this city Bangalore. As it was a Sunday, Edi office, along with the industrial estate was closed. I lingered on a bus with name plate 45A and started to explore the beauty inside the city. When you visit a new place, the experience is always exciting. You just move on and on until you touch the last end. The anxiety of catching a new vision didn't make me realize when an hour passed and the last stop still didn't turn up. I thought may be it wasn't a city bus but an inter city bus. I asked the conductor to stop.

I stepped down and began to find which area I was in. The road was dotted with small, white cottages with flat roofs and low wooden sacks built out with doors or windows. I scratched my dark hair. "I have to get back," I murmured to myself."

Two men walking by, carrying lines of slender, silvery fish came towards me. They had thick beards and wild unbrushed hairs.

"Which place is this?" I asked in a soft frightened voice.

"(English) gott-illa!" One of the strange Kannad men said refusing to know the language.

I gazed around quickly, trying to figure out where I was, but found no other soul in sight. I felt like slapping myself. Nevertheless, what to do and where to get transportation was an issue for me. I walked 2-kilometers but did not find an auto.

I looked up and prayed to God, "Please God, save me. This is the last time; I promise I won't repeat it again ever, amen."

A wish from heart always is fulfilled. It was a true prayer, which God didn't reject. I saw a cab coming. The cab driver had a nose the shape of a turnip, and eyes sunk so deep I can't imagine how he sees well enough to drive carefully. But then I wonder it was none of my business. I needed to get back to my hotel.

My hair rose up when I discovered that the area which I was a near by village 25km away from Bangalore. I promised myself not to make any such mistake again. While I was coming back, I noted the names of each place I was passing through in a diary so that next time I don't get lost in the city.

"How much Bhaiya," I asked for the expenses.

"One hundreds fifty only", he said.

"Hey —!" I cried out in surprise not because one - fifty was a bigger amount but some how I couldn't find my purse in my back pocket jeans. "Where is my purse?" I glanced around, getting ready to run to find the purse. "Where to go and search? Where will I find it now?"

I searched my jeans pockets again. "I don't believe this! I lost my purse."

"I had all the money inside," I screamed. It was tough to convince the cab driver that my purse was really stolen. I don't know when someone slide it out from my jeans. I did not feel anything. As soon as he found that, I am with empty pockets, he started speaking bulshit in Kannad.

He might be abusing me in his language. I went to the hotel and described the story. As that person had my deposit money with him, he paid the expenses.

I jammed the money into free hands of the cab driver indicating him to get lost. He was a jerk. He dropped the money into his pocket and moved but for me now it was very difficult to survive. I called my dad and asked for a money order. As my ATM was also in my wallet I couldn't get cash transfer. He immediately transferred money through a known agent. I took ten thousand rupees and planned to leave and go back home.

Did such a small thing scare me? I mumbled to myself. So why was I running? What will happen about the internship program? What will I tell Waghela sir?

Life was difficult, full of troubles, sorrows, and pains but I thought that I have to stand back and remain confident. I have learned never to blame a day because these bad days teach us many things. Never to blame a person especially who helped me move out of that village. A series of head bursting questions evolved in my mind and stopped me from leaving. The experience was a true learning for me.

The next week I went to see the place, which I was going to share. He was living in an 8 x 6 room along with two room mates. The place was too small but I had no other option. They use to pay 1200 bucks as rent per month making a division of four hundred each. Now they had me to share the expenses.

It was difficult to fit in the place. I asked them where I should keep my luggage and their indication was clear towards the 8 x 6 room. I shifted my luggage and continued with my plans. I went to the industrial estate, where in I met Mr. Rao who was handling the cluster development program. They provided knowledge about textile machineries, its use, as well as operation. In addition, they even offered me to be a part of the textile expo 2008-09.

The training process was going fine and I had many things to learn from it. However, the place where I was living was giving me a problem. I had not stayed in such a place before. For the first time, I experienced how people live in small houses, with limited sources. The pain could only be experienced by feeling it. Space was not at all a problem but with a rod inside my knee, it was very difficult to shit in an Indian bathroom.

It was so uncomfortable that everyday I had to visit to the nearby ***Pay and Use*** municipality bathroom in need. The thing screwed me to such extend that I started living in a hotel paying 200 everyday instead of 400 bucks a month in that place. I went to Arvind mills and had a word with Anant Mishra, production in charge. He showed me the process and asked me to clear whatever doubts I had. When the cluster development program equipped me with the knowledge of latest machineries and equipments, Arvind mills provided me information about the process as well as cost analysis of the project.

It was my 15th day in Bangalore as well as a Sunday too. I was in mood to watch a movie. When you don't get a company do not get upset. Sometimes one should spend quality time by being alone. While I was in Bangalore, my other batch mates were enjoying lavishly in China. I was thinking about them, when suddenly a call from an unknown number buzzed. The number was not from India. I picked up to see who it was.

"Hey who's this?" I asked

"It's an emergency? Do you know what we say '*chuna*' in English"

"Oh, Abhinav, how are you man? How is the trip going?" I asked urprisingly.

"I said it's an emergency... asshole"

"*Chunna..!* The one we apply on walls or the one we apply on people"

"*Chutiyeh...* The one we apply on pan", he screamed furiously in intervals.

"Hemmm..., what we say yaar." I thought why he is asking such a weird question.

"That's what I'm asking you. Quick, there is a problem," he said.

"Why what happened? Is everything okay?" I thought he was joking but he didn't sound so.

"Nothing dude, Jai Randhawa has been caught with his '*120 tobacco masala*' and that '*Chune ke tube*'. The cops have arrested us with the charge sheet of carrying drugs with us.

"Oh my God, you are in big trouble. But where is Prof. Yagnik who was with you guys?"

"We came to Hong Kong for entertainment all alone."

"Thank God I did not agree to come to China otherwise I would have been in the same jail." I giggled.

"Please boy. It's not a time to joke. Get me an idea how you to make these Chinese understand about the Desi tonic."

"Let me think... (Pause). Limestone...! Ya, we call it limestone."

"Cool yaar! That was I looking for, now bye."

"Wait Abhinav, listen to me first. Go to the cops and tell them the meaning of tobacco masala as well as the use of limestone in it. Make them taste and ask them to test the product in laboratory. Show them your Edi I-card. Anyhow, make them understand and get out of it."

"Thanks boss, you saved us today."

"And ya kick Jai's ass from my side for keeping indefinable items in a foreign country."

Later on Abhinav called me again and told that they were released after 2 hours of inquiry. I skipped half an hour's movie but then continued with my program. After the movie, while I was moving I met a student.

"Hey"——! I called a curly haired boy, dressed in an outfit with t-shit made of black and brown layers, which appeared from the backside.

"Hi! This is Dev. Can you tell me where I will get a bus pass?" I asked the stranger.

They looked me over from head to toe, rating me on a general scale of first impression.

"You have to move towards the railway station. There, you will find the main bus stop of the city. There you will get an I-card issue counter." He said.

"What is you name?" I asked

"Vineet and this is my room mate, Deepak. We study here itself in

Jain College. Nice meeting you."

"Okay, so you stay in hostel? I am completely new to the city so don't know anybody. I have come straight away from Edi, Ahmedabad," I said.

"No. We live at Banshankri in a rented tenement. So what's Edi?" He asked for the word new to his ears.

"It's Entrepreneurship Development Institute of India. I am here doing my internship in Arvind mills. Everything is fine here but the place I live is pathetic." I said making bad expressions about the place.

"Where do you stay?" Vineet asked

"Hemmm... 114, Somaya Apartment near Chinnama koil forth crossing, fifth lane, Bannagiri. That is what the actual address is."

"Cool yaar! You have mugged up."

"I had to by heart it so that I don't get lost."

"What kind of place is it? Sounds strange!"

"If you guys don't mind can I ask you a favor?"

"Yes of course. You can ask for sure."

"Can I share your place for fifteen days? I know it doesn't sound cool that a stranger is asking but I am in a problem. I will pay whatever the rent is."

His grey lenses widened in surprise. They thought for a while and then...

"This is my Id proof if you wanna give a look"

"Okay you can come," they said after a close glance on my Id. Here is my mobile number and the address. You can bring the luggage today itself."

They nodded and went away.

When you do well to others, God is surely going to do the best for you. I had never imagined my life to change so rapidly. I shifted my luggage and came to the new house. It was a huge bungalow with all the facilities providing a *heavenly effect* to me. That was the unexpected comfort I was receiving. There was even a bathroom with a commode equal to the size of the room where in I was previously staying.

The place was amazing. Soon Vineet, Deepak, Mohit and Akash became good buddies. I could work for more hours on my report and came up with a fantastic idea.

"Let's party today in the name of a brilliant business idea I have developed", my voice contained happiness and a lot more enthusiasm while talking to Akash.

"What is it? Even I want to hear", said Vineet who banged from behind.

I started speaking solemnly. I wanted to start a kind of business, which was equivalent to food or health or sex. A business related to appearance always makes good money, any consumer in the world spends most in appearance related things like clothes, shoes, accessories, life style products and many more such things. Human mentality likes something different and they wish to have something unique. It is more about fantasy and I would like to fulfill their needs.

"So Dev sahib is on an astonishing track. Aren't you copying IDEA'S bottom line "Think different –think *hatke*"

"No Deepak I have a different concept", I said. We always liked to fulfill our own wishes and demands; I wanted to look forward providing unique and innovative wears to people fulfilling what they like to have, want to have, and will have to have. I will provide the first kind of designer studio in Ahmedabad.

"Bangalore gave you this idea and starting in Ahmedabad is unfair", Akash made a silly comment. "Is it some mall concept or what?

"That needs cash and lots of fund" said Deepak.

My idea revolves around a studio where consumer will have what they want to, what they like to have. I thought to name it MDW, which indicated men's designer wear whose mission would be to provide affordable quality men's designer wear to the fashion conscious."

"The bottom line of your idea is to go towards the fashion industry isn't it, Deepak said"

"My store will help lot of consumers who have to visit city like Mumbai and Delhi for designer lines."

After a heavy discussion we dispersed for a movie along with dinner from my side. The restaurant was newly opened. Akash scanned the menu card and ordered for every one. Days passed faster than leopard running.

With the data collected from Arvind mill, I got an idea about the RMG industry. The business plan was fantastic and all my room partners helped me to complete my project with their innovative ideas. I completed the detailed project report, which I had to submit at the end of the semester. Waghela sir would be amazed to look at my work. The textile expo helped me a lot to gather contacts, within a short span of time. When I returned to Edi, everybody was talking about his or her experiences. Foreign visitors had that China bug all time inside their mind to murmur upon. Some of the south Indian people who did not go to China came up with interesting project reports. One such was Tibin Mukeshjiander who wanted to start a sea crab business in Kerala.

"In which field you are preparing your project?" I asked.

"It's just a diversification to my family business," Tibin said listlessly.

"Ask him what his father does." Ajay said.

"He is into fishery business right now," said Tibin.

"So, what are you planning then?" I asked.

"When my father catches the fisheries a few crabs get stuck in the net. The idea is very simple. He will enjoy the fishes and pass on the crabs to me"

"Oh... Fuck off man"! You are such a creep, I said to Tibin while he was still laughing on his lame joke.

Even Abhinav also came out with a unique concept of opening a khadi store in Jodhpur. Vivek was still working with his project.

While others were busy with preparing the report, I was seeking something else to pass my time. With that idea, I went to Kalpesh's room. Because of God's disgrace, he suffered from physical disorder in his left leg. His room was on the ground floor. When I went inside, he was chatting with somebody. I saw the id, James_peter@yahoo.com. He was chatting with a Philippina girl.

"What you doing brother?" I asked.

"Nothing, I am chatting with a Philippina girl." He said.

"Pretty Hemmm...!" I whispered. That girl on the internet has a charm of a fairy when she wakes up from sleep.

"Wanna see her nude on web cam?" he asked as if he had that x-ray software through which he could make the invisible, visible to my eyes.

“That will be your kindness if you could do so!” Abhinav said who was also with me.

He placed a bet of 100 bucks if he succeeds. Abhinav agreed accepting the bet. He thought Kalpesh was creating hype. After that, he showed me his true magic. His hands started working faster than any normal person on the keyboard. A One twenty word per minute was an amazing speed. I was looking at his accent. This boy has already worked in a call center so no one could find the person behind the id. Finally, when he succeeded, Abhinav had to give him his reward.

The experience was indigestible for Abhinav. Meanwhile I disclosed the incident with other friends, Abhinav now thought of a prank... He took his laptop and created a yahoo id in the name of **Jenny loves getting nude@yahoo.com**. The id was attractive and easy for us to get Kalpesh attention. As soon as the id was created, he sent a friend request to him to chat on it. Kalpesh, who was desperate on the other side, got excited to get the invitation. And then the conversation started.

Jenny: Hi James.

James: Hey honey how you doing. How did you catch hold of my id?

Jenny: from the Philippines, chat room.

James: Wanna get naughty with me?

Jenny: that is why I am here.

James: but why are you desperate? Anything special about me?

Jenny: It's tough to find a macho man. Hope you are?

James: you have come to the right place honey. Wanna have a glimpse of my biceps? Turn on your web cam. You will get a proof about my masculine physique.

(Abhinav accepts his web cam request and stares at what he was showing.)

Jenny: wow man! What biceps you have. I would really like to feel the pleasure.

("This idiot is showing the picture of Brad pit that came today in the Times of India newspaper," I laughed)

James: It's your time to show something. Why not have a glimpse of the beauty inside you.

Jenny: Oh! You are making me Horne.

While Abhinav was chatting, everybody came to know about the Bakra of this evening. There were 16 people betting on a lame guy for just 100 bucks which Abhinav lost. On continued insistence, Abhinav turned his web cam on, and send him a request. When the request was granted, he made Kalpesh so desperate by squeezing his chest to give him the effect. Abhinav was a man born with a waxed body. It was enough to make Kalpesh's pants tight. He then started to show his ass. At no single point of time, he gave a hint about the prank. Switching off the webcam Abhinav began to chat again.

James: why did you switch it off?

Jenny: I just wanted to look at you. You are wild and I could feel your senses. When you are so tough, how tough would be yours...!

James: Wanna have the pleasure. Look at it.

While the prank was going on, nobody had thought this would happen. Kalpesh got so much excited that he started masturbating. It was a sin for the boys to look at it. That was the cheapest prank. Abhinav again switched on the web cam showing his squeezed chest giving an effect to excite him more.

Suddenly he got a glimpse of few students. He switched off the yahoo account and then disappeared. Everybody had a good laugh at him. I went to his room showing no indication that I knew about the prank. He was nervous and did not talk with me much. That night he didn't even turn up for dinner.

It was 9:30, closing time for dinner. Mess was the only option he could satisfy his hunger. He came out of his room looking here and there. Everybody made themselves disappear in different places to see his reaction.

When he found nobody in the main corridor, he started moving fast towards mess. Abhinav who was standing on terrace, called me to depict his position. When finally he was in the mess with his plate, everybody rushed with a hungry note. All of us wanted to have dinner with Kalpesh. He was shocked looking at the gang of boys who almost banged unfortunately for him. I don't know what the moral of this story was but everything that happened there was at the cost Kalpesh.

"Hey Kalpesh, how are you?" Abhinav asked. "why are you late for dinner?"

"Was not hungry, so came late," he said.

"You [illegible] weak Hemmm...! Please serve him some tonic." Abhinav shouted.

"No thanks. I am okay," he said looking downwards.

"No man. You need it after all you have worked so hard." Tibin said.

"Oh fuck off you assholes. What you are trying to show. Have you created a big joke by viewing me nude?" Kalpesh cried loud.

He became another puppet for people's entertainment. Nobody cared about how the other person would feel about it. They just wanted to crack a nut for their pleasure. He cried loud leaving his food aside. When everybody experienced that it was a height of making fun of a person, everybody left the place leaving Kalpesh all alone to regret about the incident.

While the groups created by the college for different specialization there were, groups created formed among the students also.

1. Family business management.
2. New business enterprise
3. Agri-entrepreneurship and
4. Service management

The universal brothers were all happy with their sisters and they had nothing to do with the other students. The south Indians had their own community as a group and they did not have any concern about others. A new group prevailed breaking the SAGAR'C. Vivek and Vishal who always wanted to be with Modi, Gaurang, and Chirayu formed their own union.

They were now called the communist with only three members of the SAGAR'C.

Vanshi, Vivek, and Vishal went so far from us that despite being in the same hostel, it took days to catch a moment of conversation. There were many like me who did not want to be related in a group.

We were free to move anywhere we liked. But many times, I would feel myself left alone away from the masses.

FINAL ACT

Time fades away only memory stays

The fourth semester started with a mark of deep stress.

It was time to submit the detailed project report. Everybody feared that if a rejection was announced he or she will have to work upon the financials again.

A few made the project for the sake of presentation. But, for me it was my last chance to convince the financial institutions to fund my project MDW. I had really worked hard for the project and now it was show time. Abhinav and I were the first duo who was done with the project report. An idle mind will always go in the wrong direction. But when you have self-control inside, you can never let wrong things happen. We used our brains to do something great in Edi so that every time we entered the college premises in future, people remember our deeds.

While Abhinav had a zest for fame, I also got some touches of his nature. His Satyagrah got him no food and nothing else. I thought to organize a meeting with the eighth batch students as I was missing them very much.

My thoughts were small and limited but Abhinav was totally opposite to me. I haven't thought that far. He thought a master plan to gather all the alumni at Edi for an entrepreneurial meet. Alumni meets are very common in colleges but at Edi, such a meet never took place. May be nobody took an initiative. The idea was to gather a pool of successful passed out Ediots who could share their business ideologies with us giving a hint of how professionalism works in the real world. May be they could keep us as a trainee if we actually wanted to go into the same field. May be they might act as a prospect customer for those who already had a sound family business. May be for those who haven't thought of anything may get a fruitful business idea.

Benefits were many but how to avail those benefits was an issue. I was confused to find so far the mixed nature of my batch mates. For the first time now, I saw ninth batch as one and united, working for a cause. We gathered contact details, email addresses, phone numbers of the entire alumna's searching through data from the library.

Plans and presentations with expenses worked out came from future Einstein's of Edi. After reaching every possible alumni we got a list of 430 ready to share their day with us.

Ganpati sir (our librarian), scheduled the event with a program of two days. The budget was high so it didn't have an approval from the director. The proposal was worthy but its accomplishment was doubtful. The institute refused to spend thousands for just a meet, but then sharp brains work under pressure. The greed of fame is present in every entrepreneur and I thought may be if we provide them a taste of fame it will be possible for us to fetch funds in return.

Soon an email buzzed in the busy lives of the entire alumni's requesting them to spare two days for the meet which was going to be held. The excitement of meeting old buddies after a couple of years is something like reunion of two brothers who were lost in a circus and suddenly they found each other alive. Days came back when I could again meet Sinish, Puneet, and Viral. They brought the same environment, which they left with their departure on the last day.

Along with toasting the *Patyala's* they inaugurated the 37-china town and started the blunder game of money. Those members of the hard core drinkers rally again came back to the mood because that night DJ Parin was going to make a blast with his new look. That fat ass got thin with waist size just 34". May be the lavishness at Edi could only be felt at Edi itself.

Out of all whom I was missing to see were Sahil and Anchal. The duo actually tied a knot. I wondered how it could happen after Sahil puked vodka on Anchal breasts and she slapped that night. It was strange for all of us but later on he revealed his inside story.

Sahil spoke

What I did to that girl was something like raping a blind woman but actually, she opened my eyes. That crackling slap didn't leave me even in my dreams. One horror night when moon vanished like *Mr. India*...

"Sahil... Wake up" a roar evolved inside my room while I was sleeping. I woke up scared rubbing my eyes to adjust to the darkness. I was alone in my house and I did not know where the voice came from. It was harsh, cruel, and full of anger.

Who is there? Who is there inside my room? I shouted holding the water which was going to drain from inside. You cannot frighten me like this in the middle of night? That's unfair... are you a ghost, a witch or...

"Shut your mouth! *Mein bhagwan hu*, I am the almighty.

Heee hee (lol)! What a joke? Hee... I cannot control my laughter? Hey Bhai come out of the curtains.

Do you think it's a joke going on? You stupid creature. I am ashamed of myself that I created you.

Are you serious *Babaji*? But why me? Have I done any thing wrong?

"I order you to rush immediately and ask for forgiveness from that girl Anchal on whom you puked the vodka that night".

"Shall I go now"? I asked in fear.

"Immediately", He grooved

I was so scared that I immediately took a flight to Mumbai and rushed straight to Anchal's house to apologize my guilt.

Ting tong... (The bell rings)

"Please give only two liters milk today Bhaiyaji, mom is not there", a soft sleepy voice floated in my ears. She actually didn't see who was there.

"Oh honey"... opps sorry, sister, opps Anchal, I am so sorry for what I did to you at Edi. I should not puck the vodka and if I did that by mistake I should have apologize to you. I know it's very late and why now at this time but you know I have came all the way from Ahmedabad to accept my guilt.

"What the hell are you doing man?" she shouted throwing the milk vessel in anger.

"Please forgive me... please... please... no you can't do this to me...SORRY",

"Fatak!" I got a tight slap from my brother while I was still dreaming about that girl.

What you were doing idiot? My brother screamed at me like anything.

Oh, shit! Was it a dream? I asked myself scratching my head. But, whatever it was, I got a lesson. After a few days, I went to Mumbai for some business stuff. There I met this charming girls Anchal to whom I apologized for my deed. When she came to know about that crazy dream, she had a great laugh. I was feeling so light from heart like a gas balloon.

After that meeting, we guys became good friends again. We met often with every conversation I made; I got the color of love for that girl. I proposed her and to which she said, "Yes."

That night the party went smoothly again with every glass of *Patyala down de throat.* I sat with Sinish to share about the thing, the division of students, I never believed him. Sinish now was the CEO of *Virasat* group a well-known brand in the metal industry. There was something in the eighth batch students which never let the energy level down.

They came with a spark and enlightened the whole atmosphere. With the meet, I met many new people and heard their success stories, how they developed themselves as successful entrepreneurs. Among all, there was one face, which I will never forget.

His name was Sumit Grover owner of Vinod Internationals.

He helped us to carry out the alumni not only financially but also served his purpose as a true Ediots. He cracked many jokes and shared incidents of his past which made us realize that it was only we who had a joy ride with all the fun but later on when Sumit depicted his story inside Edi; it was made clear that all the credit goes to the place itself. Some people feel awkward to talk and be a friend to a person elder to his age, but I did not feel any difference. He had already lived the time a few years back where I was standing but today also, the spirit hasn't shattered inside him.

Among all Shiven was the person who received marvelous benefits from the meet. He went to China to experience a holiday, but there he came out with a fantastic business plan of opening a wholesale business in Ahmedabad to supply Chinese PDA cell phones. The supply will be totally to corporate houses that provided mobiles of cheaper range as bonus or incentives to their employees. He even signed a memorandum of understanding with a cell phone manufacturing firm.

The idea was a dream for him but when he showed the business plan and the financials worked out to Sumit it became a reality indicator when Sumit promised him to finance the business plan and give the idea a direction. When you ask the qualities of a real entrepreneur, being spontaneous in decision-making was one of the many.

Everybody left leaving behind a ray of hope and encouragement among the students. While others started settling down strong vibes of separation could be felt as if something was wrong between the communist's. I had never seen Vivek sitting alone reading a book. He was calm, tensed and was reading the course material. When I went to look at him tears occupied his eyes. Vivek was tough and I never saw him crying. I asked the reason, but he neglected me asking me to leave.

I could feel a cold war taking place among the communists.

"*Some one is not in a good mood today,*" I said and sat beside Vivek. "Got something you want to talk about"?

"Nothing, I want to study alone. Will you please leave me alone," he said being tensed.

I know it's not about the DPR stuff. "*Speak it dude, you will feel lighter*". Vivek remained so quiet that I wondered if may be he isn't here at all. I leaned forward so that I catch his eye. "You aren't okay". Vivek's eyes narrow. He got to his feet's then turned his back to me.

"Jesus"— look at me buddy.

I stood up too. "Hey boy, you are a strong man. Look at me". When he faced me pain drew every line of his features tight. I forced my self to think about the situation he was in.

Vivek spoke

A group of six was moving very smoothly at Edi. Vanshi, Vishal, Gaurang, Chirayu, Modi, & me. Vanshi & I were very close to each other. We were best friends but our friendship became a black mark for the other group members. Things started getting wrong during our internship period when Gaurang got attracted towards Vanshi. He started calling her on daily basis. Miles long chatting became a matter of enjoyment on phone.

Gaurang, who was a male chauvinist, right from his graduation days in S.D.Burman College, did not have any female friends as close as Vanshi. The care she showered on him was of a group mate. I don't know why people perceive a girl's favor as love or attraction. A screwed up looser will always think the other way round. He started thinking that Vanshi was interested in him. This matter was discussed with his best pal Vishal.

Vishal pretended to be girl's psychologist started pumping the love factor in his heart for Vanshi. Nevertheless, the main point still occupied their minds regarding Vanshi's inclination towards me. They considered me a play Boy who was spoiling that girl's life. I was shocked to know that it was spoken to her in order to separate us.

"But why telling bad and unjustified things to her regarding my character,"

"May be they both were worried about that girl," I said interrupting in between his story.

"But why getting me down." They even convinced Modi that I was playing with her life and he should stop her.

"What the fuck are you talking about"? Is that real, I said surprised. I grabbed Vivek's arm as I stared at him in shock.

"This is nothing in comparison to the blunder that happened with me," he said.

"Is a blunder still going to happen yet," I laughed.

In between psychos: Niriksha (childhood friend of Vanshi) encountered them who were also of the same category.

"A psycho"? I questioned.

She was a psycho because she was having an affair with a married man who used to make a total fool of her and enjoyed all the pleasures.

Even she thought that these people were very good doing the right thing by warning her friend. However, Vanshi and I shared everything so how could this thing have remained hidden. One day I asked her regarding the tensed mood she was carrying, and she told me everything what all other members of their group were saying about me. I was hurt on hearing this. I could not find out the reason why my friends were saying those sorts of things. When the vacations got over, I straight away asked the three about the issue. Nevertheless, they simply denied, changing the course of talk saying, "There cannot be any type of couple in a group"! In addition, if Vanshi and I are having something, we should admit that and leave the group.

I brought Vanshi and other boys together and wanted togetherness but I didn't knew Gaurang thoughts were so cheap.

It hurts when you are blamed unnecessarily. The whole group was upset for about a fortnight.

"So did you find any conclusion, I asked.

Then, Hundreds of meetings, with no conclusions off course!!!

Gaurang, Vishal, & Modi were having something more in their mind. They went to Jaipur to tell the whole matter to Vanshi's Parents. They spoke all sort of garbage regarding Vanshi and my relationship.

"What are you talking man. Did they go to her place," I shouted in anxiety.

"Yes, they were crazy." Human beings are like snake. You feed them, love them, nourish them, but at the end they will only turn upon you.

Her father informed the complete matter to Vanshi's cousin who stays in Jaipur. I came to know when her cousin Ekta gave me a call to discuss the matter. She knew that Vanshi and I were friends and the other boys were creating hype.

"Thank God Vanshi's dad didn't believe those guys otherwise he might have fucked you up completely", I said.

He came to college and gave written complaint regarding the three boys who tried to spoil their girl's image. For security reasons, he even took Vanshi along with him saying that it will not be safe for his daughter to remain in hostel.

"Oh! That's why I didn't see her in the campus since last 15 days".

Her cousin wanted that those three creeps to be debarred from the college. She and her brother went to Prof Bakshi to talk about the issue. Ekta's brother was politically strong and so he started threatening the three boys he will file a case against them. When they did things well for the girl, they did not think that the situation would come back negatively towards them. Ekta's brother called assistant commisnor of police Mr. Gayakwad to take the three boys in remand but later on it was found that the commisnor was one of the close political relative of Modi.

The matter was dumped but not for me. Vanshi was spotted with Modi and company more than half a dozen times in the city even after all this. I am broken because my best friend Vanshi and other family like friends, all exploited me. No one tried to understand me.

"That is sad", I whispered.

"You know who was behind those Mirchi mails", he asked.

"Who was he"? I questioned in excitement to know the truth, which was hidden since last 10 months.

'Mirchi mails' was the sole idea of **Gaurang Agrawal.**

I knew... I knew that it was his cheap idea. No one at Edi is as smart as him.

He used to receive these sorts of mails in college when he was in Delhi. Therefore, he got the idea of writing Mirchi mails to everyone at Edi. He took Ankul, Shiven, Ronak, & Abhinav into confidence.

Then after some time, Chirayu also came to know about all this.

I was searching for the culprit right from the time when all of us received the first part of Mirchi mails.

I short-listed some batch mates whom I thought were capable of writing such things. Gaurang was one among those. I got a list of IP addresses from the computer lab. Then I started monitoring the computers of the short listed batch mates.

One day I hacked the system of our respectable Gaurang Agrawal. I showed him the mail, which he saved. Gaurang then accepted the fact that he is into all this. I once promised that I would raise the mask from the so-called Mirchi Seth. But now I feel very low and bad. One of my close friends was a culprit, the one who always used to tell me that he just hates hypocrisy and dual-faced persons.

But now he was one of them.

His story was pitiable but I could not do anything for him.

I departed suggesting him to forget the past and concentrate on the project. I felt pity on him. He left us to enjoy the grapes with the communists but wasn't aware about the sourness.

While sitting outside the jury member's room I was concentrating on what to speak. It seemed like confessing a crime infront of your

Hitler dad. The fear of being judged can lead to either confidence or nervousness. I could realize my ass would disrupt by the pull of contrary forces. After a few minutes, the panel of jury members called me to proceed with my presentation. They already had a copy of my report.

"You have 15 min, Devendra!" A jury member uttered. "Shoot"

The jury included director Edi V.G.Patel with mentor in charge Prof. Vaghela and chief finance manager Mr. Dinesh Pandya from ICICI bank.

I was about to speak but could not remember what I have mugged up. It felt as a heavy lump as if my voice has passed away rapidly. Visuals of my visit to Bangalore started to revolve around my empty head. The professor gave me a glass of water and asked me to relax.

After a few seconds there was a question fired. Speak about MDW. I concentrated on the word as if never heard before. I forced my mind to gather the right words to shoot upon the juries.

"MDW is a chain of men's designer wear apparel. The store is meant to surprise the target customers with the affordability of the merchandize."

I said with a confident note in order to convince the jury about my project. I could now recollect the knowledge, which I collected during my internship period in Arvind mills, from the **TEXTILE-EXPO** as well as from the cluster development program.

The answer gave me a lot of relief and then I began to speak what I have already prepared.

I am interested in garment industry and that specified men's designer wear manufacturing. The unit resembles manufacturing of men's wear like designer shirts casuals and jeans from fabric to finished product.

There are many parts of ready-made garments like women's wear and kids wear but I would specifically go in MDW with its own retail stores.

"So what is fashion design according to you"? Waghela sir asked in order to take things out.

Sir, Fashion design is the applied art dedicated to the design of clothing and lifestyle. They are accessories created within the cultural and social influences of a specific time.

"Have you any plans of out sourcing your requirements for MDW"?

MDW will offer an extensive selection of quality, value-priced apparel, and accessory. By concentrating on apparel with limited fashion risk, the store hopes to offer a substantially greater number of sizes, styles, and colors than its competitors do. The store will source its fabrics and accessories from *Prem Kalp Agencies*, Ahmedabad (Cotton, Prints), *H.E. Abdul Azeez*, Chennai (Leather, Knitted Fabric), *Pasari Inc.*, *Kabadi Shankarsa*, Bangalore (Made ups, Accessories and Artificial Jewellery) through strategic alliances. The manufacturing and packaging will be sourced from *New Madhupura market*, Ahmedabad.

Looking at my confidence Waghela sir was proud.

Mr. Dinesh who came as an ICICI bank representative was keen on testing me. After all, he was going to finance my idea. He fired many questions one after another.

He even told me that the plan was like a dream and it was very tough to cope up with the current market in reality. But looking at my financial and my presentation style he was quiet impressed.

Specify your strategies! I would like to see how efficient you are in your project?

MDW0690 has aimed to be known as the destination for the people who wish to buy designer wear at a reasonable price. The stores of this company will be named as MDW0690. This name will appear as a number plate of a vehicle.

Segregating the name, MDW stands for Men's Designer Wear and 0690 with the emphasis of 69 is meant to cash on the fact that the number is related to ***'Karma'***, which titillates the mind of the prospects.

The Tag Line: ***"Your keep in the wardrobe.***

For every answer I gave them, they had another question. But finally, I left the room with a loud sound of clapping from the jury members. I walked out of the room, past the reception and the other sell-shocked nervous students waiting outside for their turn to come. The project was extraordinary. Mr. Dinesh sanctioned 60 percent loan on the cost of my project. Now it was all upon me to arrange the rest forty percent and get through my project.

Not only Gaurang, but also Apurva, Vivek and I got the same appreciation which I got. The day of our joy were getting over.

It was just fifteen days left for the ninth convocation to take place. While the students of eighth batch were starving for a moment, we people felt the last days equivalent to months.

The feel of separation did not give any emotional setbacks because they had no meaning. I even thought as if we people were forced to live together. It felt like a jail and now the release date has been sanctioned.

The journey was a combination of fruitful and ginger spice melodies, which not only entertained but also made me learn and experience different things.

The real taste of life isn't in sweetness.

It's the Papdi chat that gives the best spice flavor.

After a year's story being narrated to you, can you find the difference between the seniors and my batch mates?

When the seniors acted as sweetener, the rest acted as a chilly Masala making a perfect combination. Both left a different mark behind the story with distinguish attitudes.

Chilies only leads to burning Ass..es in the morning but still people include them to experience the harsh taste.

Days neared the convocation Day and a notice was placed for us regarding the convocation.

Shashi Ruhia from *Essar group* was going to come as a chief guest and bless the entrepreneurs. It was a warm feeling inside to see Mr. Ruhia for the first time. Such entrepreneurs always become an inspiration to ignite our energies.

The nominations for the Bharti student of the year started. Eighteen people were selected whose GPA was highest among all. I wasn't in the list not because my grades were low. A period spent with the dukes resulted into low attendance and my name was out. Though the causes of absence were a result of the bad company but I didn't know God would repay with side effects like this.

Students voting were a part in selecting the best student.

History speaks here that whether its elections or voting for a leader or a best student, politics cannot be separated. The communists always wanted that Gaurang win the award. They applied every political thought to gain votes. My cousin Rajesh was also one of the nominees so he deserved my vote. The poll ended after each student has given his or her vote.

It was the last day.

Ankur Nahar made a movie about the days we spent and he tried his level best to turn us emotional. He arranged a quick get together to share his work.

The movie was fascinating with played pictures and events. He wanted us to cry and feel the last moment because after that night everybody was going to leave.

It was a fantastic work by him. But after the lights were on I found that a few had even bunked and moved away. The others were in a sleepy mood, stretching their revolving chairs. It meant that everybody was tough to hold the tear but I think that emotion had lost its value.

I wanted to speak something to the class. I stood up and came forward.

Friends,

It was a good time for me with you people. A year has come to an end and now when we have to push our lives towards the practical world again, I hope you all do the best. But, I have just one regret in my mind.

I started the trend to humiliate Sameer Bhai and then the SAGAR'C continued to the end.

We fucked every ones ass in the name of joy but finally see, "what we have achieved."

"Grim looking face," where in it would be more suitable

to go home rather bearing each other. It's the outcome of those acts we performed, that now we want to get rid of everyone and everything.

I wished to experience the same factor that had united ninth batch, what the alumni's saw during the meet. But now it's really tough.

You might be thinking what a crazy person I am carrying totally impractical stuff inside my head."

After Some days, when the leaves turned and cold came, every now and then I would rise in every one's mind like a tide. You will even forget me, my name, my voice, who I am, and who I am to you, but this impractical stuff will remind you of me because truth cannot be forgotten.

It's quiet, tonight. Weeks have rhythms all their own, and the craziness of a Saturday or a Sunday stand in direct contrast to a dull Monday. I can already tell: this will be one of those nights where I bunk down and actually get to sleep.

I left with a sad note.

That night Chirayu moved away first, just after the convocation. He did not even bother to say good-bye. No body cried because their tears were more costly than the emotions experienced. The communists were not happy because Bharti award went to Suvendu an NGO guy. When they all went out to chill in a group, the other group of universal brothers occupying the girl gang too went invisible sharing the last moment. Everybody else slept at one giving a careless note.

The next morning when I woke up, half of the batch mates had gone. I packed my bags and took Rajesh to the station to drop him.

I didn't want to turn around and look who else was left to go. I moved to my home exactly opposite of the enthusiasm, which I showed when I stepped on the first day in Edi.

Edi acted as a best place where I not only experienced all the phases of a movie but also equipped me with a huge mass of knowledge base.

I thought to came out of the mood of brooding, because from tomorrow

"The journey towards success was going to begin"

Epilogue

Fashion is a common word but MDW has given it a new meaning. No body has thought that a young entrepreneur of 23 will blast men's fashion market with his MDW - 'Spice' flavor. Let us have a peep into his collection tonight.

MDW - 'Spice' collection is made up of shiny denims, dirty retro washes, denim/Lycra, and Various styles from detachable to multi-pocketed ones. In addition, the non-denim Collection includes flat front trousers in triple blends of cotton, nylon, polyesters, and linen, which will add a charisma towards your life.

It's tough now to doubt MDW'S exclusivity. So, let me call upon the man behind the show Devendra Rai a successful entrepreneur from EDI Ahmedabad.

MDW 0691
YOUR KEEP IN
THE WARDROBE
IF YA THINK
THIS HURTS-
TRY MISSIN' OUR
NEW COLLECTION

It was difficult for people to grasp my rapid successes but what fascinated them the most was my collection, which I threw for display during the Delhi fashion week. The collection was not only different but people around were amazed to see this new *Avtar* of MDW. It was a surprising decision taken by Nilesh to move for designer casual outfits. He was working very hard and what he brought out was not only going to buzz the market but also was going to increase the TRP of MDW.

Delhi... fashion week !

My idea was taking shape and Nilesh efforts were giving men's designer wear a new definition in the fashion market. We buzzed the market in the same way we decided with our new offerings.

Natural fiber

MDW has enhanced its product offering with the introduction of the Two-Tone linen Collection. Drawing inspiration from the international focus on linen this season, the store claims to add value by giving linen a special finish that lends it a two-tone hue.

Designer Jeans

Cozy range of jeans, is interplay of global fashion trends, comfort and quality for the youth.

The trendy cuts in broken twill and dirty denim Lycra fabrics in sporty college casual styles have been shaped for enhanced fit.

A few years after... LONDON fashion week:

They mastered the art of entrepreneurship and have turned their dream into 150 men's designer wear studios all across the globe.

Ladies and gentlemen, let us call upon stage the handsome hunks of EDI, Ahmedabad, Devendra, and Nilesh with their new denim collection for die-hard denim freaks.

This time MDW – '*Masala*' include Mobile Pants, and new stretch fabrics, which adjust with body movements.

The Mobile Pant is a wrinkle-resistant trouser and is in a temperature-managed fabric with custom fit, which expands the waistband.

For, *Die-hard denim freaks* its time to chill out. MDW has expressed denims in different textures, embroidery, and abstract prints.

The tinted sandblasted jeans in green, dark blue or the dirty indigo are tailored to match with their shimmer shirts.

Success stories are many but you might not have encountered a story like this. It has been few years they are into this business but I personally feel like years have passed away. MDW has come up with an exclusive designer wear and paying a few thousands is worth it.

It was a warm welcome given by the Americans. Especially the host who couldn't stop praising the concept of MDW.

I again stepped inside the moods of prosperity.

I started moving towards the ramp taking small steps to feel the honor, which I was going to receive. The feeling was great and the greatest part was my success, which brought me here. However, it wasn't a one-man show.

While I was walking, there was one man beside me. He was NILESH

PATIDHAR my fashion designer. Do you know who he was?

A senior from eight-batch who applied detergent on Ritesh. When we again met on the ENTRA-PLEXUS meet, I discovered many things and out of the many discoveries, Nilesh came out as an unexpected hero. We joined hands to give MDW a shape with the support of ICICI bank.

Ms Lena, host of the event handed me the mike to speak some golden words and my experiences. To my surprise, she asked about my life at Edi. It was at her request that I started speaking solemnly.

Hello every one...

It is my pleasure to serve you best outfits every day when you come to my store. When we have reached on such a stage where in your expectations are increasing day by day I hope you are satisfied with our offerings. A few minutes before while I was moving towards you my mind jumped to my past reminding me the struggling period, which I experienced. It was tough to carry six downfalls in a period of four months for my first venture. But to turn into the wind meant driving another roller coaster up and down. For one blessed moment the sail went still. There was a hope that a day will come when I will show my dad that his son wasn't a 'fake coin'.

I rose again like an ant towards the path, which Waghela Sir (my Edi mentor) showed me. I promised myself never to turn back. Whether it was a struggling period or a downfall, I thought to apply, my friend Shiven's ideology taking life as a daring adventure or nothing.

Twentieth is a very crucial year of our life. Either we move towards our carrier or we become a fool to take it lightly. I experienced both these stages but at the end, it was my mind that has started thinking about

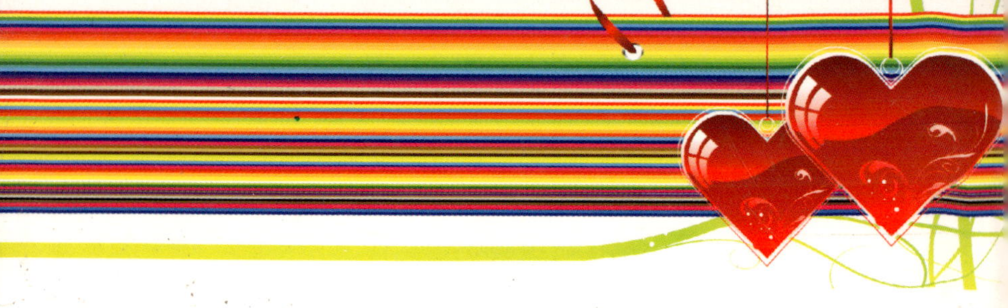

... "Its fun -- spicy-- all the ingredients of action, adventure, humor, witty conversation all rolled into one superb dish of fiction waiting to be read and enjoyed!

Ladies and gentlemen, welcome to

Patyala down de throat

Dev : Whatever happens cannot be blamed on God ...Then onwhom???

Mom : Is this a hostel or a hotel? - Surprised!

Vivek : Guys! Eyes on jasmine. She looks pretty with a perfect ten. Long hair, sharp nose, milky white like she is made up of cream- Vanilla...aaah!

Vishal : Jasmine likes you Dev. Trust my theories - 'The Inside Story.'

SAGAR'C : We are nuts! Crazy and dangerous. Dare you mess with us Dev !

Mirchi Seth : This is the first Edition of *GARAM MASALA*

'Tujhe mirchi lagee to mein kya karun?'

Dudes : Welcome Dev, to the dark side - Mehfil @ EDI

The Director : What will happen If I reject your business plan, Dev?

Life : At some point you will have to be serious about your future Dev !

Will Dev meet his Success????

Watch out for season's best flavor, just a hundred bucks away!!

Cover I Chandra Prakash

www.chandraprakashmohata.com

ISBN 978-93-80349-16-9

9 789380 349169

₹ 100